DETROIT PUBLIC LIBRARY

T5-AFU-691

"Now, you know if you come in here, you're going to get your hair wet."

Ivy could see the desire in Jonathan's eyes and she was ready to join him. Loosening the knot in her robe, she slipped it off, letting it hit the floor.

Stepping forward, she whispered, "That's okay. It will be worth it."

Jonathan immediately slipped his arms around her waist when she joined, pulling her against his hard body, and then gave her bottom a light squeeze.

With Ivy's arms wrapped around his neck, he stopped the water flow and guided her to the back of the shower where he sat on the granite bench and pulled her onto his lap. He kissed her lightly on the lips and gazed into her dark brown eyes.

Ivy rested her forehead on his. Lowering her eyelids she said, "I love you."

Both stunned and touched, Jonathan continued studying her before confessing, "I love you, too."

Sealing his statement, he kissed her wildly.

CHANDLER PARK LIBRARY
12800 HARPER
DETROIT, MI 48213

FROM THIS MOMENT

SEAN D. YOUNG

Genesis Press, Inc.

INDIGO LOVE STORIES

An imprint of Genesis Press, Inc.
Publishing Company

Genesis Press, Inc.
P.O. Box 101
Columbus, MS 39703

All rights reserved. Except for use in any review, the reproduction or utilization of this work in whole or in part in any form by any electronic, mechanical, or other means, not known or hereafter invented, including xerography, photocopying, and recording, or in any information storage or retrieval system, is forbidden without written permission of the publisher, Genesis Press, Inc. For information write Genesis Press, Inc., P.O. Box 101, Columbus, MS 39703.

All characters in this book have no existence outside the imagination of the author and have no relation whatsoever to anyone bearing the same name or names. They are not even distantly inspired by any individual known or unknown to the author and all incidents are pure invention.

Copyright © 2011 Sean D. Young

ISBN: 13 DIGIT : 978-1-58571-383-7
ISBN: 10 DIGIT : 1-58571-383-x
Manufactured in the United States of America

First Edition

Visit us at www.genesis-press.com
or call at 1-888-Indigo-1-4-0

DEDICATION

This book is dedicated to my one and only sister
Shirlonda Nicole Taylor
"Red"

ACKNOWLEDGMENTS

Oh give thanks unto the Lord for He's been good to me. I'm so grateful for His mercy and kindness toward me.

I would like to thank my wonderful circle of friends who prayed, supported, encouraged, read and re-read and even sat down side by side with me, sacrificing their precious time to help me. You are so special and my life has been enriched because you're truly my friends.

Alicia Thomas: thanks for suggesting that Ivy and Jonathan should be together in the first place.

Deborah Schumaker and the Genesis Press Family: Thank you so much for this opportunity to share my story with the world.

CHAPTER 1

How could I have been so stupid?

Ivy, her back slumped over her sofa staring at the ceiling, asked herself that same question for what had to have been the hundredth time.

She'd been a wedding planner for more than five years and had created some of the most stunning events the Chicago area had ever seen. Yet, she never imagined her own marriage would take place in an all-night wedding chapel in Las Vegas at 2 a.m. A ceremony she only remembered in snippets that joined her in holy matrimony to Jonathan Damon. Of all people.

Ivy didn't think Jonathan was a bad guy; from what she knew of him he seemed pleasant enough. He was certainly easy on the eyes. He personified tall, dark and handsome, with his rich dark chocolate skin, soulful brown eyes, clean-shaven face and sensuous mouth.

Funny. Much of last weekend's events were a blur to her, but she did remember her encounters with that mouth.

She'd had quite a few business dealings with Jonathan, the co-owner of Magic Moments, one of her most preferred vendors. It was an upscale banquet facility in Taylor, Indiana, a town thirty minutes from downtown Chicago. She and Jonathan had shared several meals together with her family, because his brother Marc was married to her sister Rose. And that was it. She didn't know a whole lot about him.

How had she gone to Las Vegas for a convention and come back . . . married.

The annual Association of Wedding Industry Professionals convention took place over a four-day period every winter in a different city. It showcased the newest wedding looks, trends and designs that would premiere during the upcoming spring bridal season.

The association also recognized leaders in the industry and awarded them.

This year's convention had had extra buzz, for the association was looking for a local wedding planner in three major cities—Chicago, Los Angeles and New York—to host their new reality TV show, *Here Comes The Bride*. Each week the local planner chosen for these special one-hour episodes would help ordinary couples have a platinum-style wedding on a budget.

Ivy had worked on her video entry for the Chicago spot for weeks, deliberately trying to go with something as imaginative as possible for the wishes of the fictitious bridal couple. She'd been thrilled to learn she'd made the final five. The winner would be announced at the awards banquet.

Even now, Ivy couldn't help smiling broadly as she recalled hearing her name called as the winner. "Ivy Hart," the association president announced. It was surreal.

Her heart had pounded in her chest as Jonathan happily embraced her against the background of audience cheers. She remembered thinking this must be how it felt for an actor to win an Academy Award.

She'd gone to the stage to accept, alongside the portly, fifty-something veteran planner who'd won the top spot for New York. Within minutes they were joined by the final winner, a tall, thin young man with bottle-blond spiked hair, who would host the L.A. show. The three of them spontaneously shared a group hug, to the delight of the audience.

What a glorious moment that had been. It was, however, what happened *afterward* that had her in a near-catatonic state.

Now she sat in her living room, alternating between closing her eyes in despair and opening them to glare at the evidence of her ill-thought-out marriage.

Who was she kidding? She'd given her action no thought at all. She picked up the large white envelope that had been given to her at the chapel and pulled out a photograph.

Ivy pressed the photo to her chest, face in. She closed her eyes for a second and said a prayer before looking at it, hoping against hope that it would be some other woman standing beside Jonathan. Of course, that desperate measure was fruitless. There she was, wearing the new royal blue chiffon gown she'd so carefully selected to wear to the banquet and a big smile.

Placing the photo aside she reached inside the envelope again, and this time took out a marriage license.

Tears leaked from her eyes as she studied the document yet again. This piece of paper legally linked her to a man she knew little about and who was now her husband.

The last item inside the envelope was the ring, a plain gold band she vaguely remembered Jonathan purchasing at the chapel's gift shop. It was supposed to be a symbol of love, faith and devotion between two people. In her case none of this was true.

Ivy felt a steady throbbing in her right temple. She jumped up and quickly pulled the curtains closed to restrict the brightness of the sun. She needed to think things carefully through.

What would she tell her family? His family? *Him?*

She didn't want anyone to know about what she'd done. As for what she'd have to say to Jonathan, Ivy had no clue, but she had to come up with something fast. She'd invited him over this morning to talk about their situation. He'd be there any minute. Slowly she got to her feet and went to clean up. She'd made a terrible mistake.

How could I have been so stupid?

Jonathan Damon deliberately parked his SUV down the street and out of sight just in case Ivy Hart was looking out for him. When he knew what he wanted to say he'd pull up closer to her condo, but right now he needed time to get his thoughts together.

Jonathan flipped the visor over the steering wheel down, then opened the plastic cover to reveal the lighted mirror concealed inside it.

Did his embarrassment show? Maybe if he studied his reflection as he rehearsed, it might help him figure out what he was going to say to his wife.

"Wife." Just the sound of the word coming off his tongue made him nervous. He dropped his head.

What have I done?

It had taken him thirty minutes to get to his destination; a trip he usually made in half the time. Ivy lived in the same condominium complex in Shaker Village that his brother Marc had, at least until he married Rose.

Jonathan continued to stare in the mirror as though his speech was written there. Yet, he still couldn't get past, "I didn't mean to hurt you."

Marc had always warned him about acting on impulse. Jonathan had wanted to get to know Ivy, but he may have just destroyed any real chance of getting close to her...by marrying her, of all things.

But he had to face her. He could no longer avoid seeing her because no amount of rehearsing could prepare him for whatever it was awaiting him.

He got out of his car, remembering that his attraction to Ivy started several years before at a relative's wedding. The bride, Ivy's cousin, had hired her to coordinate the event.

They'd talked during breaks at the rehearsal and exchanged numbers. The day of the wedding, he'd been sick with some kind of flu thing, but, fortunately his duties as the best man were pretty much over by the time of the reception. He'd thought it was sweet when Ivy had called him the next day to make sure he was okay.

Her youngest sister, Lili, called her an ice queen, but Jonathan didn't believe it.

How could a woman who created some of the most magical, breathtaking fantasy-themed weddings to be seen in the Midwest not want a romantic relationship for herself?

After that initial meeting, he and Ivy often had a chance to work together on the details of ceremonies and receptions held at Magic Moments. Some of their conversations concerning mishaps, blunders and outlandish requests gave them an opportunity to share a laugh.

Then they'd kissed.

He would never forget the way she felt in his arms the evening of the Magic Moments grand opening. After the event ended and all the guests, photographers, critics, prospective brides and the local newspaper reporters had gone, Ivy had come to congratulate him.

And they had continued to work together. Jonathan loved the passion and excitement he saw in her. He imagined Ivy showing those same emotions toward the special man in her life, and more than once he daydreamed of being that man.

Many times Jonathan had to caution himself to keep his distance from her as they discussed room setups and other details. The scent of her perfume and the memory of her soft lips against his made him want to move closer; to touch her.

Yes, she had fine physical attributes, but he wanted to get to know the real person on the inside. But Ivy would never allow him to get that close. Except for that one kiss, it was always business with her. And then, three days ago, just like that, they'd gotten married.

Once back home, he'd left countless voicemail messages and when she didn't return his calls, he decided to wait to hear from her.

He understood the situation was a lot for her to process and he would never forget the astonished and reproachful expression on her face the morning after when the young woman from the front desk of the hotel called his room to inquire if the newlyweds needed anything.

How had this happened? Ruining her life certainly hadn't been in the plan. He'd gone to the convention in Las Vegas to network and to discover new trends that would help his business thrive. Running into Ivy at Midway Airport and learning they were on the same flight had come as a pleasant surprise.

The usually efficient, businesslike Ivy Hart was surprisingly relaxed that afternoon. He thought her comfort level had to do with them being acquainted and right away he began flirting with the idea of transforming their relationship to something more personal.

Ivy had offered to guide him around the convention, suggesting the seminars which would benefit his business and the ones to stay away from. He appreciated this. It was his first time there, and she knew it.

They went to many of the seminars together.

Jonathan felt buoyed when she invited him to sit with her at the awards banquet, and of course he accepted.

He'd never seen Ivy so excited and happy. She simply glowed with pride when she won the honor of co-hosting the association's first reality TV show.

Once the awards were over, there was a media blitz. Ivy had asked him to come along with her as she did her interviews and posed for the cameras with the winners from the other two cities. She even introduced him to the show's producers. Everybody wanted to get a picture of the newest reality TV stars and Jonathan was proud of her.

They went to an after-party sponsored by Maggie Sottero, one of the biggest bridal gown designers in the United States.

The music was bumping and the dance floor was filled with people. The party was well attended with others standing around talking or sitting at little tables.

Jonathan and Ivy had been celebrating all night, dancing, drinking and having an all-around good time. He noticed that after a couple of drinks, she was a different person.

Jonathan was so enthralled with Ivy that when he suggested they get married, he was only half joking. He just knew she was going to throw the rest of her drink at him, slap him or laugh in his face, but she stunned him by saying yes. He knew he should have known better than to go through with something like that, something so permanent - but they were living in the moment.

This moment.

He'd reached her door. She opened it before he could ring.

CHAPTER 2

He'd seen her look better. Her eyes were red, their lids swollen. The once sleek and gracefully statuesque young woman with the luminous mocha skin and perfectly coiffed hair now wore a pair of gray sweat pants and a white tank top. She was barefoot, her hair pulled back in a simple ponytail.

He wanted to reach out and caress her cheek, comfort her for the hurt he'd caused, but he knew they had to talk it out first.

"Are you okay?" he asked, taking a step closer.

Ivy stepped backward. "I will be once we get this farce of a marriage dissolved."

Jonathan sighed deeply before taking a seat on the couch. His heart dropped when Ivy sat on the love seat instead of next to him.

She leaned forward. "I hope to God you didn't tell anybody what we did."

"Why would I do that?"

"It was *your* idea for us to get married and *you* were in much better control than I was. So I'm not sure what *you'd* do." Ivy got up from the love seat. "I know *I* didn't tell anyone."

Jonathan leaned forward, resting both elbows on his knees. "No, Ivy, I didn't tell anyone. And as for me being in control . . . well, I didn't think getting married was a bad idea at the time . . ." He stopped, but then gamely started again. "And if you want to know the truth, I still don't. But I don't think you share my sentiment."

"You're damn right, I don't," she shot back. "I'm a thirty-four-year-old responsible businesswoman, and there I was in Las Vegas carrying on like I'm Britney Spears. And just like Britney's this marriage was over as soon as it started, but, unlike Britney's, nobody's going to know about it."

She moved closer.

"Look, Jonathan, I've done the research, and in order to get this marriage annulled I'd have to go out to Vegas. I'm supposed to be meeting with the producers for the show, and with the day-to-day business operations of Hearts and Flowers, I just don't have the time right now. But as far as I'm concerned, it's already annulled, just not officially."

Hope. Some hope. Ivy wasn't going out to seek an annulment right away, which meant he had a chance to get her to change her mind. He found he liked the idea.

Ivy extended her right hand. "Can we shake on this or something? I just don't want your family or my family to know. I don't want *anybody* to know."

Jonathan, rising to his feet, stared at her hand, and then his eyes moved up to her face.

"Do we have a deal?" she said.

Jonathan accepted, but he held her hand in his rather than shaking it. "Yes, we have a deal."

He felt her try to move away, but he didn't want to let her go. He held fast, looking down at her small hand enveloped in his large one. The two hands looked good together.

She pulled her hand away.

"We need to forget everything that happened between us," she mumbled, turning away from him.

Jonathan raised an eyebrow. Had she sounded a little breathless? Had she felt something when he cradled her hand? He walked around to face her. "Ivy, I can't forget. I'm not even going to try. Can you honestly tell me that you can?"

She stared at him.

He nodded. "I didn't think so." He turned on his heel and headed for the door. Once there, he paused and turned around.

"Is there anything I can do for you? You look like you haven't eaten or slept in days."

"Gee, ya think?" Ivy said sarcastically.

The telephone rang, and it was just as well; he didn't have anything more to say. As he opened the door, he said, "You have my number. Call me if you need anything,"

Ivy watched him until he was halfway down the sidewalk. She closed the door before she answered her phone.

"Hello."

She recognized the voice instantly. "Vee, are you coming in today? We're so anxious to celebrate your win, but we didn't want to plan something if you won't be here."

Ivy managed a dry cough. She didn't want any visitors, especially not her sisters. Not right now. She might blurt out her secret.

"No, Violet, I'm not coming in. I appreciate you guys wanting to do something for me, but I'm not feeling too well." She coughed again. "We can celebrate another time."

"Do you think you need to go to a doctor?" Her sister sounded concerned. "It's been, what, three days since you came back with this bug?"

Ivy had to get Violet off the phone quickly. She sounded curious as well as concerned.

She feigned an uncontrollable cough before speaking. "Violet, I need to call you back later."

"All right, but we'll call you tonight to check on you."

This time Ivy made a sneezing sound. "Okay." She put the phone down, but not before she heard her sister tell her to get something for the cough.

Ivy threw herself onto the couch. She hated lying. Now that she didn't have to worry about her sisters calling back, she had another concern and it was even greater than the first. She knew that Jonathan and his brother Marc, her brother-in-law, were almost as close as she was with her sisters. Would he really be able to keep a secret from him?

CHAPTER 3

Meeting with the executive producers of the reality show, the Wedding Industry Association and the Wedding Channel turned out to be more nerve-wracking than Ivy had thought. She had no idea that there would be so many people involved. As soon as she arrived, she learned they planned to tape her first episode in a couple of weeks.

That episode would be the premiere of the nine-episode series between the three planners airing in the fall. Hers would be titled "Here Comes The Bride—Chicago with Ivy Hart".

She was thrilled that they added the tagline she used in her video presentation for her show: "Where wedding dreams that last a lifetime begin."

Entries poured in from wedding hopefuls in a casting call from the Chicago area newspapers, national TV ads and The Wedding Channel website. Finally the producers decided on the three couples from the Chicago area whose weddings Ivy would be arranging.

A large notebook filled with photos of the first couple, their bios, and, finally, their wedding wishes was given to Ivy. She had to study them and prepare a wedding timeline for a meeting with the bride and groom. This would be held in the next week. Ivy's plans for a platinum wedding on a shoestring budget would have to be condensed into a one-hour episode.

Ivy concentrated on the facts and tried not to get overwhelmed with a lot of the details. She concerned herself with the things for which she was responsible and let the producers do the rest. She just hoped the couple wouldn't be difficult.

Ivy said her goodbyes and assured the producer that, if she had any questions, she'd be in touch.

Super Bowl Sunday was a big event in the Hart Family. It always had been. A large number of their extended family and friends showed up to eat, watch the big game and have fun together, while some of the women who didn't enjoy football spent their own time catching up with the happenings of their families.

But Ivy wasn't at all pleased when she pulled into her parents' circular driveway and saw Jonathan's black SUV parked against the curb. Still she knew that asking that he not be invited would only raise suspicions, especially since he'd been attending the annual event for several years.

She hadn't spoken to him since he'd left her home more than a week before. Communicating with him would only be a reminder of their carelessness . . . and a reminder of her eager responses to his hands and lips that night in Vegas.

Ivy jumped out of her dark blue BMW and went to the back to retrieve her contribution to the party. At home, she'd prepared a pasta salad and three-bean casserole, and on the way over she'd stopped by Subway to get some sandwich platters to go along with all the other food she knew would be served.

She walked around to the back door, leaned inside, grabbing the platters first. When she suddenly heard Jonathan's voice, she nearly hit her head on the roof of the car.

"Need some help?" He stood behind her.

His immediate appearance made her suspect he'd been watching out for her.

Ivy stepped back, straightened her spine, turned and handed him a sandwich platter. "Thanks," she said before pulling out another one, placing it on top of the first.

She continued to remove the food from the back seat of her car.

"I can take one of those bags, so you won't have to carry so much," Jonathan said.

"I picked up the last of it. I think I've got it."

Without saying another word, she strolled in front of Jonathan wondering if he was watching her as they walked into the house.

Ivy prepared herself to remain calm and not become paranoid. Nobody else in the family knew she was Mrs. Jonathan Damon. She wanted to keep it like that.

As soon as they walked through the door, everyone inside yelled, "Surprise."

Ivy almost dropped her casserole. Her heart pounded like she had just finished running the Chicago Marathon. She was already being paranoid, but to meet with such a response when she walked in with Jonathan . . . she didn't know what to think.

Lili took the casseroles from her and motioned for Jonathan to follow. The two of them disappeared into the kitchen.

Her other sisters, Rose and Violet, ran to her and threw their arms around her. "Congratulations, Vee!"

Ivy's shoulders went as stiff as a new pair of jeans. What the heck was going on? Her sisters had already taken her to dinner to celebrate her hosting gig, and their parents had come, too. Why were they congratulating her now?

She scanned the room to see who was there. She hadn't seen her Aunt Elizabeth or her Uncle Joseph at a Super Bowl party in years. She was just as surprised to see her cousin Irene, who always had an excuse for not coming. Ivy couldn't believe so many people had come out. Her cousin Destiny was there with her husband Nicholas, and family friends Vanessa and Keith sat on the couch.

Good Lord, had Jonathan talked? Ivy hugged her sisters, hoping someone would say or do something so she would know how to respond.

Before she released them, she scanned the room looking for Jonathan. Once she spotted him she raised her eyebrows, anticipating he'd recognize she needed help. "Oh, my goodness, you guys didn't have to do this."

Jonathan came over to stand next to her. He helped her out of her coat and handed it to one of her relatives before saying, "You should have seen Ivy when they called her name." He turned to Andrew, her father. "Mr. Hart, it was truly a Kodak moment."

Ivy turned to smile at Jonathan, hoping he saw the relief in her eyes. Turning back to the others, she said, "It was an incredible moment."

"I heard you guys partied like rock stars," Violet said as she walked back into the room carrying a sheet cake.

Tears sprang into Ivy's eyes. She didn't realize that Jonathan hadn't moved from her side until he wrapped his arms around her shoulders. She was truly overwhelmed by the lengths her family went to surprise her.

"Did Lili bake this?"

"Of course," her sister answered, beaming with pride.

"It's so pretty." Ivy looked at the white rectangular cake with bunches of roses in all four corners and the words CONGRATULATIONS TO OUR STAR written in the middle in purple script.

She glanced around the room at the beaming faces of her family. "You really shouldn't have. We already celebrated."

"Yes, sweetheart, but that was *our* celebration," her mother, Louvenia, said. "We wanted to mark the occasion again today with friends."

"That is, if there's any cake left over when the rest of them get here," Marc Damon said, his arm around Rose.

"I think Lili did a good job," Rose said.

"It's a lemon cake filled with raspberry buttercream."

Ivy hugged Lili. "You really outdid yourself on this one, my sistah. The roses look so real." Ivy wanted to reach out and touch them.

"You know better. They're made out of sugar paste," Lili said. "Are you going to cut it now?"

"I can so that we can serve it with the rest of the desserts."

"Wait, girls, I want to get a picture of Ivy cutting the cake," their father yelled as he rushed from the room to get his camera.

"Go on into the dining room," Louvenia suggested. "I don't think there's any room on the table in the kitchen."

Everyone filed into the large dining room area and gathered around the rectangular table, which had both leaves in and seated eight. Ivy stood at the head of the table, keenly aware of Jonathan standing slightly behind her.

She picked up the cake cutter when her father returned and motioned to cut into the cake, but Andrew stopped her.

"Wait, sweetheart." Andrew held up his hand. "Jon, why don't you get a little closer to Vee? Since you were there with her for her big win, I want you in the picture."

Ivy tried not to show anything on her face.

"You deserve this," Jonathan whispered, his lips almost grazing her ear. Ivy wanted to lean into him. She could feel his breath on the back of her neck.

"Now cut your cake," he said, speaking normally.

Everyone applauded as she cut into the sweet confection and placed the slice on an empty plate nearby. She felt calmed by Jonathan's words, and at that point all thoughts of her secret being revealed disappeared.

Ivy looked at her watch. "Isn't it almost time for the pre-game show to start?" She picked up the small plate and pinched the end of the cake. Popping the little piece in her mouth, she moved from behind the head of the table. "Let's get something to eat and watch the game."

Forming a single file line, as many as could fit in her parent's eat-in kitchen, filled their plates with the variety of foods that had been placed on the table.

There were hot dogs, bratwurst, polish sausage, potato salad, pasta salad, three bean casserole, fried chicken, chips, spinach dip, chili, hamburgers, spaghetti and meat balls and all the condiments. The beer, sodas, juice boxes, punch and flavored water were submerged in ice within three coolers that sat in various areas of the kitchen.

As soon as their plates were prepared, they headed to the family room and balanced them on their laps while gathered around the large television there, which was tuned in to the pre-game show.

Ivy took her place in line. Amid all the loud whiffs and comments about how good everything looked, she realized how foolish she'd been to think that her family's cries of "surprise!" were due to her marriage. They'd be shocked to learn she and Jonathan were married, and they'd want to know what was going on, how they'd managed to keep a courtship—Ha! That was a good one!—a secret, why weren't they living together. They wouldn't just break out in a celebration any more than people really broke out in a song the way they did in Broadway musicals.

Eventually only Jonathan, Violet and Ivy remained in the kitchen. "Can I get you something, Jonathan?" Violet asked.

Ivy stared at Jonathan. She wondered why he was still in the kitchen. He certainly couldn't fit another thing on his plate.

"I was going to get a beer." He was trying to steady his food and pick up the bottle of MGD out of the cooler that sat on the floor. His gaze went to Ivy.

"Can you get it for me?" he asked, giving her a big smile.

"Sure." Ivy reached down, opened the lid of the large red cooler next to the wall and retrieved an ice cold bottle of beer.

She handed it to him and watched as he left the room. She then picked up a paper plate filling it with food. She and Violet walked out of the kitchen and joined the others to enjoy the football game.

Jonathan couldn't keep his eyes off her. He discreetly watched as she ate and cheered on her favorite team. She was clearly having fun, and didn't seem burdened with the fact that they were married.

He'd enjoyed being with her in Las Vegas, but sharing and celebrating with her family was an honor. His brother might be the one married to a Hart sister, but the family had always treated Jonathan like one of their own.

It had troubled Jonathan not to be able to call and check on her, but he respected her wishes. After all, he was the one who told her to call if she needed anything. She hadn't, but that didn't change the fact that he wanted to speak to her in private . . . and what better opportunity than during the party?

As they finished eating, Jonathan rose and made his way through the people who sat on big floor pillows, and as he passed the card table where Ivy and Violet sat, he bent and whispered in her ear.

It must have been hard for her being around her family and holding onto this secret. It had to be emotional. Jonathan only wanted her to know that he supported her, or so he told himself.

"Can we talk for a minute?"

"About?" Ivy asked. She nervously glanced over at Violet, who wasn't particularly paying them any attention.

Jonathan replied in a slightly louder voice. "I wanted to talk to you about the special order for the table linen for the Stone wedding reception."

"Can't it wait until tomorrow?"

"No, we have to give the supplier an answer first thing in the morning."

"Shhh!" Violet said, pressing her index finger against her mouth. "Go in Daddy's office and talk, I'm trying to watch the game."

Jonathan wanted to kiss Violet. He wanted to be alone with Ivy, and she'd just set it up for him.

Ivy stared at her sister and Violet hunched her shoulders. "What? Just go in the other room and talk to him, Vee. He's just like you, talking business on the weekend." She waved them away.

Ivy dropped her fork, pushed her chair back from the table and got up.

She tossed her plate in a nearby trash can. Jonathan did the same before following her to her dad's office.

Jonathan noticed Ivy didn't bother closing the door once he stepped inside the room. They could still see everyone in the other room, and the people in the other room could still see them.

He was impressed with the décor in Andrew's office. The dark muted tones of the wall, the characteristic charm of the mahogany desk, which was filled with folders marked with bride and groom's names and wedding dates created a relaxed and serene atmosphere.

Andrew had been a wedding photographer for more than a quarter of a century. Several photos lay on top, which Jonathan figured were the proofs. He was so busy looking at the photos that he hadn't realized Ivy was speaking.

"Okay, Mandy Stone is supposed to contact me in the morning. What's the problem?"

"How've you been, Ivy?" he asked.

A crease marred her forehead. "What do you mean?"

Jonathan stepped closer to her. "I didn't like the way we ended things the other morning."

She rushed over to the door, peaked out and then carefully closed it. "Would you keep your voice down? Someone might hear you."

"I thought you said there was a problem with the Stone wedding."

"There is, but that's not what I wanted to talk to you about.

"Tell me about the problem with the Stone wedding first."

"The table linen manufacturer came back with a ridiculous price for the beaded chartreuse overlay Mandy wanted."

Ivy nodded. "I called your office and told your assistant to go ahead and place the order. Mandy's mother said she didn't care about the cost."

Jonathan already knew that, but he hadn't known any other way to get her alone.

"Good, I'll just make sure Myra ordered the linen in the morning, then."

Ivy straightened. "I hope the game hasn't started." She headed for the door, and then turned back around. "I thought we really had a problem."

Jonathan walked over to her, all the while thinking this would be his only chance tonight to talk to her privately. "I want you to go out with me," he blurted out.

Ivy wondered if he could hear the accelerated beat of her heart. He was so close, looking at her so intently, that she had to look away.

As if she didn't have enough complications in her life, he had to add more to it.

Feeling the need to pull herself together, she finally responded. "No, Jonathan. We don't make the right decisions when we're together."

Jonathan reached out, lifted her hand and held it in his grasp. "You won't even consider it?"

There *was* something happening between them; Ivy could feel it, but she didn't dare try to figure it out. Not with all that was going on in her life. She pulled her hand back and was relieved when he let it go.

"I don't know how many ways I can tell you no," she said. "Should I say it in Spanish? In Japanese? Will you get it then?"

Jonathan threw back his head and laughed. "You got jokes. Hey, as the old people say, strangers can get married, but you really should know each other before you get an annulment." He gave her his best smile.

Ivy tried not to laugh. "That is ridiculous and you know it."

Jonathan, satisfied that his story was working, tried to keep from laughing himself. So with a straight face, he continued his tale.

"No, seriously, my Aunt Rachel told me about a friend of hers who married a stranger, but before she got the thing annulled they went out on a couple of dates. Especially after she found out the man was wealthy."

Ivy frowned. "Staying with someone for financial reasons isn't love," she said.

"No, it isn't, but this woman stayed on even after he'd lost all his money."

"Really? So she did love him."

"Sure she did, and they're still together to this day."

Ivy glared at him for several moments. She doubted that the story was true. "I'm going to ask Ms. Rachel about this."

"Go out with me, I promise you'll have the time of your life," he said, ignoring her last remark.

Ivy sighed in resignation. "When do you want to go out?"

"Friday if you're free. We have two receptions planned, but its Myra's turn to supervise the events."

"This coming weekend I really need to study the portfolio the producers of the show gave to me. I'm meeting with them next Thursday. I've also been asked to write a column for the weekend edition of the *Post-Tribune* called 'Big Weddings, Small Budget'. The article will run in next Sunday's paper."

"Even more reason to relax and have a good time. And I could help you with the article," he offered, hoping to persuade her to say yes.

There was a war going on in Ivy's mind. On the one side, she didn't want anything else to do with him. On the other side, she hadn't been on a date in a long time. And if she did maybe he would leave her alone.

"This Friday it is then." She opened the door and walked out, leaving Jonathan alone. His lips curled up in a smile.

He was definitely making progress.

The phones at Hearts and Flowers were ringing off the hook. The articles, photos and announcement of the winners for the host of the reality show that were posted on the Wedding Channel website had spread like wildfire.

Brides read the article and then posted a link on their Facebook pages, tweeted and re-tweeted on Twitter and blogged about it.

In addition, the mailbox from the Hearts and Flowers website was being inundated with e-mails. Gwen, their receptionist, couldn't keep up with replying; for every one reply she received two new e-mails.

Ivy had quickly become a hot commodity. She needed to call a special staff meeting in order to put procedures in place to handle this newfound popularity.

"Man, the phones are ringing like crazy," Lili said as she walked into the conference room on the second floor of Hearts and Flowers. Placing her notebook on the round oak table, she pulled out her chair and sat down, joining her sisters at the table.

"Poor Gwen. I'm so glad she has a headset so she won't have to hold the phone between the locks of her shoulders all day. It would get on my nerves," Rose commented.

Gwendolyn Clark was a petite young woman in her late twenties with fine features and shoulder-length hair. She'd been working for the Harts for five years.

"Do you think she'll need some help?" Violet asked.

"That's why we're here, to figure that part out," Ivy responded. She opened up her leather notebook and flipped the pad to a clean sheet of paper.

"What I want to find out is if the callers are potential clients with legitimate business, or are they just people who just want to see what's happening." Ivy scribbled some notes on her pad. "We should start with the e-mails."

"First let's make sure it's not spam," Lili said, interrupting Ivy's thoughts.

"Right, that's key. The last thing we need is a computer virus," Violet said.

"If the calls or e-mails are about floral design/décor Gwen will send them to Rose, apparel to Violet, cakes to Lili and planning and all others to me."

"Our big sis is now a big star," Lili joked, emphasizing the 'r' in 'star'.

They all laughed.

Ivy blushed. "I wouldn't say all that. This is going to benefit us all."

"We've come a long way," Rose commented.

"We sure have, and it hasn't been without a lot of hard work and sacrifice on all of our parts," Violet added.

"Oh, and don't forget the fights we've had in this very room," Lili said.

Lili was a petite young woman with her father's walnut-colored skin and their mother's small build. The twenty-seven-year-old pastry chef spoke her mind, which sometimes caused problems between the sisters.

"You were always the instigator, Missy," Ivy said. She shook her head.

"I was right most of the time," Lili replied.

"Don't start, Lili," Violet warned.

"Now, girls, we have a lot of work to do. I think I may need a floral assistant," Rose said, studying the notes in her pad.

Ivy and her sisters had been business partners for more than five years. When they inherited the mansion that now serves as one of the biggest bridal retailers in the Midwest from their uncle, Henry Hart, who owned the first black newspaper in the city of Taylor, they didn't know what to do with it.

Of course no one wanted to live in it. For one, it was entirely too large. None of them were married or had children at the time, so Ivy came up with the idea that they should open their own bridal business, since everyone already had their certifications.

Ivy had earned hers from the National Bridal Service, Association of Bridal Consultants—the industry standard of wedding excellence—as well as joining the National Association of Wedding Professionals. Her ultimate goal was to become a certified member of the International Special Events Society, the hallmark of professional achievement, which she accomplished in twelve months.

Thirty-year-old Violet had earned a fashion design degree from the International Academy of Design and Technology in Chicago. With an eye for fashion, she assisted with bridal attire.

Thirty-two-year-old Rose handled the flowers, having been a floral consultant and designer with a degree in horticulture before the siblings decided to go into business together.

The sisters discussed their plans to turn the mansion into a bridal Mecca with their parents, and they were tickled about the idea. So they applied for a business loan.

The girls worked with the general contractor, tailoring the Southern-style building to their specifications.

By the time they held their grand opening, they'd transformed it into a fantasyland for brides. White wrought-iron gates, meticulously manicured lawn, towering trees and a decorative running fountain in front of the circular driveway that led to ample parking in back, was only the start of what they hoped to be a one-of-a-kind shopping experience for their clients.

When it came to the décor of the mansion they wanted classy, elegant and royal. From the white marble flooring in the foyer, crystal chandeliers, fluted columns, wall coverings and draperies to the *Gone With the Wind*-style staircase and balcony; they wanted every bride to realize their wedding dream.

They'd come a long way, but Ivy wanted to make sure they continued to live up to their reputation for excellent customer service and attention to detail.

It was important that they discussed sales figures and unusual requests, talked about any problems and/or needs for supplies, and so on for each aspect of their business.

It was usually done on a monthly basis, but with the new surge of potential business they would have to report weekly just in case they really needed to hire additional staff.

Just before the meeting was over, the receptionist buzzed in.

Ivy picked up the phone. "Yes, Gwen."

"There is a young woman on line one who said she read the article on the Wedding Channel website and she needs our services right away."

"What's her name?"

"Lauren Kabins. She's twenty-six years old and she wants to get married in three weeks."

"She wants to get married in three weeks," Ivy repeated so her sisters could hear.

Weddings with short timelines only meant a lot of rush work for them. If the client was uncooperative and unresponsive to their requests it made it even more frustrating. Ivy hoped this would not be the case with this young woman.

"Thanks, Gwen." Ivy ended the call and cleared her throat before she spoke.

Pressing the button, she said, "Good morning, Lauren, this is Ivy Hart speaking."

"Ms. Hart, I read your bio on the Wedding Channel website and I need your services right away. My fiancée is going to work overseas in three weeks. Can you help me?"

"You have a three-week timeframe?

"Yes. Can we put something spectacular together in such a short time?"

"Yes, we can, but we'd have to start planning right away. Are you looking to have a ceremony in a church or synagogue?"

"Neither. I'd like to have the ceremony and reception in the same place."

"How many guests do you expect?"

"One hundred of our closest friends and family."

"Will you have a large wedding party?"

"Eight. Two bridesmaids, two groomsmen, a maid of honor, best man, flower girl and ring bearer."

"Have you purchased a wedding gown?"

"No, the only other thing I've done is call you."

Ivy chuckled as she wrote quickly on her writing pad. There were several banquet halls that came to mind. She'd have to call Jonathan's first.

"Lauren, are you free this afternoon?"

"Yes, I'm free. Can you see me today?"

Ivy could hear the excitement in the young woman's voice. "Hold one moment; I need to check the calendar."

Ivy turned to Violet. "Can you pull up the schedule and see what we have in three weeks? I don't want to tell this young lady we can help her when we're booked solid."

"How does she sound?" Lili wanted to know.

Quickly everybody gave her the eye. They didn't want her to start causing trouble. Lili hunched her shoulders. "Hey, I'm just asking. I don't want to have to bring out the Vaseline and the straight razors if this girl is a fruitcake."

Ivy shook her head. "Anyway, Violet, what do we have?" she asked, ignoring Lili's comment.

The schedule popped up on the large screen of the laptop computer they kept in the conference room. "We have one event, the Chamberlain wedding, that Saturday afternoon, but that's it."

Ivy was satisfied. They didn't have a lot to do for Shauna Chamberlain, so planning Lauren's wedding would be a breeze. "Good, we can handle that."

She went back to the caller. "Lauren, we are available."

"Yes, yes, yes. Oh, I'm so relieved."

Ivy could hear the excitement in the young lady's voice. She nodded, confirming to her sisters that they had a new client.

"I have to put you on hold one more time, Lauren. I want to call the banquet hall to check their availability. I may be able to get us an appointment for this afternoon, and we can get started."

"I'll be right here until you get back."

Ivy put her new client on hold, and then switched to another line and dialed.

"Magic Moments, Bessie speaking, how can we help you?"

"Ms. Bessie, Ivy Hart calling for Jonathan."

"Ms. Hart, how are you today?"

"I'm great. Is he in the office?"

"Yes, let me get him on the line. Hold one moment, please."

Suddenly butterflies swarmed in Ivy's stomach. Inhaling deeply and exhaling slowly, she waited only moments before that rich baritone voice wafted through the phone.

"Jonathan Damon."

"Jonathan, this is Ivy Hart." Why she said it like that she'll never know. Of course he knew it was her, the receptionist probably already told him.

"Do you have any events scheduled for three weeks from now?"

"Sounds familiar, but let me check." Jonathan pulled up his meeting calendar on his computer. "Saturday's booked solid, but we do have the Embassy Ballroom available on Friday night. Maximum capacity is one hundred people."

"I'm not sure if the bride is set on getting married on Saturday. I'll have to find out. Do you have some time to meet with me and the bride this afternoon?"

"How's two o'clock?"

"Excellent."

Suddenly there was a pregnant pause. Ivy wondered if Jonathan wanted to say something. All she could hear now was his breathing. She couldn't say anything personal to him, since her sisters were watching.

Finally, Ivy spoke. "See you at two."

"Look forward to it."

Ivy ended that call and quickly pressed line one.

"Lauren, Saturday's booked. Would you consider getting married on Friday evening?"

"Friday may work out better."

"Have you heard about Magic Moments Banquet Hall on Broadway?"

"I've seen their ad in the *Chicago Wedding Magazine*, but I've never been there."

"Can you meet me there at two o'clock today?"

"Really? You are awesome, and quick, too. I'll be there?"

"Wait, wait, one second." Ivy stopped her before she hung up. She needed to give to her the address and directions. She hadn't met a bride yet that let her giddiness cause her to forget important details.

"Do you need the address?" Ivy asked.

Lauren giggled. "Oh, yes, I'm sorry, I got so excited. It's actually in the magazine, but you can give it to me."

"Do you have a pen so you can write down the address and the phone number? I don't want you to get lost."

"I'm ready."

"Where are you coming from?"

"Alsip, Illinois."

"Take I-80/94 east to the Broadway South exit. Drive about one mile and Magic Moments is located on the left side of the street. The address is 8215 Broadway."

"I have GPS on my cell phone, so I shouldn't have a problem."

"Lauren, I look forward to meeting you at two o'clock this afternoon at Magic Moments." Ivy repeated the name of the place and the address one more time to be sure the young woman was clear as to where they were meeting.

After she hung up, she stood. "This young lady is going to need everything."

"I don't mind last-minute weddings when they're simple," Rose commented.

"Once I meet with her over at Jonathan's, we'll know if it's going to be simple or a problem," Ivy responded, gathering her things.

"Speaking of Jonathan, when are you going to put him out of his misery?"

"What are you talking about, Rosie?"

"Marc told me that Jonathan has asked you out and you keep saying no. When are you going to go out with him?"

Ivy's stomach dropped. She hoped the horror she felt didn't show on her face. Jonathan was much closer to his brother than she thought. Would he truly be able to keep their secret? The last thing she needed was her sisters butting their noses into her affairs. The day had started out perfectly, and she hadn't thought about her marriage or Jonathan other than going to see him about a bride.

"Vee, you're not going to answer, are you?" Lili asked.

"The man has been sweet on Vee for years now. I know you guys had to have seen the way he looks at her," Rose said picking up her notebook from the table.

"Rosie, you're always trying to play matchmaker," Violet said.

"Why not? Vee's not trying to make a match or find a mate for herself, so I don't think it's a bad idea," Lili commented, turning toward Ivy.

Ivy didn't know how to answer the question. She couldn't tell them that she'd skipped the courtship and had already married the man. Nope, as soon as she got a minute, she'd get her annulment and that would cut the tie that bound them.

"He actually asked me to go out with him the other night at the Super Bowl party." She hoped the tidbit of information would satisfy her sister's curiosity.

There was a pregnant pause before Rose spoke. "Okay and did you say yes?"

Ivy gave them a smile that didn't quite reach her eyes. "Yes, I'm going to go out with him."

"Well, it's about time," Rose said, smiling brightly.

Ivy glanced at her gold bezel watch. "I'm going back to my office so that I can get a new client package. Then I'm off to Magic Moments. I'll have to put her information in the computer later."

As soon as Ivy walked out of the room and down the hall to the stairs, she wondered if she did the right thing by telling her sisters that she was going out with Jonathan. She didn't like other people in her personal business, especially her sisters.

CHAPTER 4

Ivy pulled her navy blue BMW into the closest empty spot in the massive parking lot of Magic Moments. As a business owner herself, she admired Jonathan and Marc's ambition in taking a once boarded-up building and turning it into an elegant place for people to celebrate their special occasions. Jonathan was the business manager and Marc was the chef. It was one of the largest banquet facilities in the town of Taylor, accommodating up to seven hundred people. The building had four ballrooms, The Embassy, Royal, Grand, and Chateau.

Hearts and Flowers started their partnership with Magic Moments after assisting them with their grand opening four years ago. Now the Damons were at the top of her preferred vendor list because of the diversity of the cuisine, their level of service, style and commitment to bringing a high-quality experience to their customers. Together they created stunning and unforgettable affairs.

Ivy checked the time on her dash to make sure she wasn't late. In fact the clock told her she was fifteen minutes early.

Ivy didn't want to go inside right away because she wanted to introduce herself to Lauren, so she turned up the heat in her car and waited. She hoped the young woman was timely. In her line of work there was nothing worse than a bride who didn't respect time. It could cause a wedding budget to skyrocket out of control because of extra fees for going over the allocated timeframe.

Soon, she spotted a silver Lexus 470 SUV pull into the parking lot. When the young woman locked eyes with her and smiled, Ivy smiled in return. Ivy was sure it was Lauren Kabins.

Ivy turned off the ignition, hit the locks and got out of the car.

"Lauren?" Ivy asked pulling on her navy blue leather gloves.

"Ms. Hart," Lauren responded, stopping in front of Ivy.

Lauren Kabins had a small, round face, shoulder-length brown hair and wore square-framed eyeglasses.

Like almost every other bride she'd met, Lauren carried bridal magazines and a notebook.

Ivy extended her right hand. "Nice to meet you."

Lauren anxiously accepted. "Nice to meet you, too, Ivy."

Ivy and Lauren walked side by side to the entrance of the building. "Did you have a hard time finding the place?"

"No, and it only took me forty-five minutes to get here."

Ivy pulled her coat collar closer to cover her exposed neck. "Let's hurry up and get inside. It's freezing out here."

Ivy enjoyed watching the animated expression on Lauren's face as she marveled at the elegantly furnished foyer when they walked through the large glass double doors.

The champagne and taupe colored walls brought charm and matched the sparkle of the gold chandeliers, original oil paintings and antique furniture in the hallway that lead to the oval shaped lobby. It was surrounded by a beautiful winding staircase on each side adorned with white silk flowers and tulle.

"This place is gorgeous," Lauren commented, taking off her winter hat while admiring a large floral center-piece on the table in the lobby.

As Ivy walked over to Lauren, Jonathan came around the corner to meet them. "Good afternoon, Ivy."

Ivy gave a generous smile. "Jonathan, I'd like you to meet Lauren Kabins. Lauren, this is Jonathan Damon, one of the owners."

Jonathan offered his hand. "Nice to meet you, Ms. Kabins. Congratulations on your engagement."

Lauren accepted Jonathan's hand. "Thank you, Mr. Damon. This is a lovely place."

Releasing her hand, Jonathan glanced back and forth between Ivy and Lauren. "Ladies, follow me and we can get started."

Ivy walked behind Jonathan and Lauren. As she watched Jonathan interact with the client, she noticed the swagger in his walk.

She admired the way his shoulders fit his gray suit jacket, and his posture was that of pride and profession-alism. He exuded confidence, and there was nothing about his body language, eyes, or the way he spoke that indicated a personal relationship between them. He was all business. And she liked it.

Jonathan stopped in front of the ballroom door. "I thought we would have our meeting in the ballroom that's available for your date."

Lauren looked over at Ivy for approval. "That's fine with me. You come highly recommended by Ms. Hart," Lauren said innocently.

Jonathan gave Ivy a big smile. "Thank you, we try to please."

Once he opened the double oak doors, Ivy heard Lauren gasp.

Even empty, the Embassy ballroom was stunning. The high vaulted ceilings projected a sense of openness and comfort. Shiny brass chandeliers throughout, two marble bar areas and a hardwood parquet dance floor that covered the entire length of the room.

The lonely table in the large space had been setup with a diamond white pin-tucked table cloth and paired with diamond white, brushed satin bag-style chair covers and a purple sash with a diamond chair cover brooch to hold it together.

Jonathan assisted Lauren out of her coat and placed it over one of the other empty seats at the table. He offered her a seat, pulling it from underneath the round table. Once she was seated, he did the same for Ivy, before taking his own seat next to her.

Lauren looked around the room, and then inspected the table that had been set with clear charger plates with gold beaded trim, Waterford crystal, beautiful flatware and white bone china.

"This is gorgeous," Lauren said, gently rubbing the see-through gold lamé table overlay.

"We keep a display table to give the clients examples of table setting styles. We change the look every other week to give it some variety." Jonathan explained picking up several leaflets about the facility, handing them to her. "All of our events come with butler styled passed hors d'oeuvres, so we can check that off the list."

Since Lauren had a short timeline, Ivy wanted to find out her plans and expectations. "Lauren, how many guests are you anticipating?"

"About one hundred."

"Do you have a budget?" Ivy needed to know how much money she had to work with so she could make smart decisions when planning the wedding.

"My fiancée told me to get what I wanted?" Lauren giggled and then pulled out a folder with a protective cover.

She handed it to Ivy. "I've written down my wishes and gathered photos of dresses, cakes, flowers and wedding favors."

Ivy placed the folder between her and Jonathan so that they could scan through it together.

Flipping the pages, Ivy gave Jonathan a quick glance to make sure she he was keeping up.

Closing the cover, she turned her attention back to Lauren. "Wow, this is a very detailed plan. Are any of these requests negotiable?"

A big grin grew on Lauren's face as she moved her head from side to side. "No. I want every one," she said with certainty. "My fiancée said I could have what ever I wanted, so I'm going all the way. You only get married once, right?"

Ivy looked at Jonathan again, hoping his facial expression would reveal what he was thinking. Hopefully, he thought the same as she did . . . Lauren Kabins was spoiled.

Both Ivy and Jonathan responded in unison. "Right."

"Are you sure you want to stick with lime green and peach for your wedding colors?"

"My fiancé loves green and I love peach, so I just thought they would look good together."

Ivy thought the combination was hideous, but she would keep her opinion to herself. Instead she asked, "Do you have an accent color you'd like to add?"

"Whatever you think is best."

Jonathan picked up a Magic Moments menu and scanned the food list on the page. "Now let's talk about your menu options."

Lauren interrupted him before he could go any further. "I'm going to leave that up to you and Ms. Hart. I don't have time to choose. I've given you a list of the things I like, so if you could work with her, she can tell me."

Ivy gave her most professional smile. "Of course he can. Jonathan and I can pull together a proposal giving you two choices for the entire day from the information you've provided to us. Give us forty-eight hours. After you've reviewed the proposals and chosen your favorite, we'll execute."

Lauren pushed her chair back from the table. "That sounds like music to my ears. I can't wait."

She inhaled deeply before releasing it. "Thank you both for meeting with me. I'm relieved and happy that I've got competent people to help me."

Jonathan stood first, and then assisted Ivy with her chair. "We're going to do our very best to meet all your wishes."

Lauren picked up her purse and slung it on her arm. "I have so many things to do before the wedding and the move. By the time we get married we will have only one week to make sure the apartment is empty."

"I'll keep in touch. I'm glad you were able to see the ballroom," Ivy replied.

Lauren glanced around the room once again. "Me, too." She looked back at Ivy and asked, "When do I come in to see you again?"

"I'll e-mail you with the proposals. If you agree, you will need to come to my office to make your selections."

"We will need a deposit to hold the date," Jonathan said as a reminder.

Lauren sat back down, opened her purse, and retrieved her designer wallet that matched her handbag. Removing her silver Cross pen from the holder, she flipped up the flap covering her checkbook. "I'll write you a check for $2,500 now and we can discuss my balance after I see your proposals."

She scribbled on a blank check, tore it out and handed it to Jonathan.

She stood to her feet again. "You can give the receipt to Ivy. I need to leave now. I promised my fiancée that I would meet him at the jewelers. We're picking out rings today."

Ivy pulled out several pieces of paper that had been stapled together and handed it to Lauren. "I'm sorry, Lauren, I should have given this to you when we started the meeting. I completely forgot. She handed the young woman the papers. "Here is some information on my company for your reading pleasure. Something so you can get to know what services we provide. There isn't a price listed for my services because I have to review your notes and make sure we can meet all your requests with the current staff that I have right now." ·

Lauren nodded. "I understand. I'll take it home to review it."

Ivy extended her hand to her newest client. "We'll discuss coordination fees once you've reviewed the proposals. And if you have any questions, please don't hesitate to call or e-mail me. It was a pleasure to meet you, Lauren."

Lauren accepted. "Likewise." She reached over and offered Jonathan a hearty handshake as well.

"Let me walk you to your car," Jonathan offered.

"Thanks, Jonathan, but I can find it."

"No, I insist." He helped her with her coat and then turned to Ivy.

"Don't leave just yet. I wanted to talk to you about a planning schedule."

Ivy re-took her seat. She picked up Lauren's wish list, which seemed more like a wish book with all the pages that were in the folder. She and Jonathan definitely needed to work quickly with the requests Lauren gave them; they were going to have to use their precious time to their advantage.

When Jonathan returned he found Ivy with her elbow on the table and her head propped up with her right hand, her eyes closed. The room was quiet and he figured she took the opportunity to relax. His brother told him that Rose couldn't stop talking about the increase in business since Ivy's win.

He didn't want to wake her, so he quietly removed the chair from under the table next to her and sat down. A smile touched his lips as he gazed down at the relaxed expression on Ivy's face. It was so different from the way she'd looked weeks before. He studied her features carefully.

With her eyes closed and hair pulled back, the light cover of makeup on her café au lait skin made her look angelic. It reminded him of the night they made love in Las Vegas, but that time her hair was loose, full and free.

As he sat quietly watching her rest, Jonathan slowly regained confidence in his decision to prove to her that their marriage could work. He realized he had a long way to go in order to convince Ivy that saying 'I do' was worth it.

Slowly, her eyes opened and Ivy sat up straight.

Jonathan scooted closer to her. "You look tired. Do you want to go over this stuff later?"

Ivy placed her hand over her mouth to cover a yawn. "We better get started." She picked up the folder, quickly skimming through the pages again. "This is a big request for such a small window of time."

"You're right, but we don't have to go through it here. You can go home, rest for a while and I can come over later. We may even be able to complete it tonight."

"Sure, we can work on this tonight. Come over at about seven."

Jonathan hadn't realized he was holding his breath until she responded. His eyes twinkled and his smile turned into a full grin as he lifted himself out of his seat. He was relieved that she didn't turn him down, because, after all, to her it was business. But for him, tonight was yet another opportunity for him to get close to her. He wasn't going to blow it; he was going to make it count in his favor. And if he was lucky, Ivy wouldn't mention anything else about an annulment.

Placing his hand lightly on her shoulder, he said, "Go home and get some rest. I'll see you later."

Ivy stood. Jonathan picked up her wool swing coat from the back of the chair and held it open so that she could slip it on.

Ivy picked up the folder and held it securely to her side.

Jonathan slipped his arms around her shoulders. "You're not too tired to drive, are you?"

"Oh, no, I'm fine. I really just wanted to rest my eyes a bit. I'm rejuvenated."

Ivy looked him in the face. "Jonathan, did you see that list?" She shook her head at the long list of things the bride wanted.

"Sure did. The woman wants everything and the kitchen sink in three weeks."

"Where are we going to find plaid chair covers?" Ivy wondered why the young woman picked something so uncommon and hideous.

"Who does that?" Jonathan shook his head.

They both laughed, and Ivy shook her head as she moved away from the table. "I've got to stop by the office before I go home, so I'll see you later."

CHAPTER 5

Jonathan sifted through the many take-out menus in his kitchen drawer. He had no idea what Ivy's favorite foods were, so he settled on ordering from his favorite Chinese restaurant. He gave the girl his selections for pickup, since the place was on his way to Ivy's house.

Jonathan lived alone in a two-bedroom apartment on the far west side of the city. Unlike the stereotypical messy bachelor, he'd neatly decorated his place with neutral and earth tone colors. He had custom black leather furniture, a home entertainment system complete with surround sound and a big-screen plasma television.

One bedroom served as his home office, but with a daybed, just in case he had an overnight guest.

A masculine king-size bed with black and tan bedding was the focal point in his bedroom.

He'd gone home to take a shower and change out of his business suit into something casual for his evening with Ivy. Just as he was about to step out of his slacks, he heard the buzzing of his cell phone. He glanced over on the night stand where he'd left it and could see the light from the screen. But he ignored it and continued to undress. Taking off his pants and underwear, he dropped them in a cloth bag with other garments to be laundered.

Walking from his bedroom to the adjoining bathroom, he twisted the knob in the shower, testing the warmth of the water before stepping under the powerful spray.

After taking a quick shower, he got out, wrapped a dark blue bath sheet around his waist and went to find something to wear.

Jonathan didn't deny that he wanted to impress Ivy, give her a glimpse of his personal style. After standing in front of his closet staring for longer than he would have liked, he decided on a pair of black jeans and white button-down shirt, black cardigan and his black cowboy boots.

Because he had dry skin, he grabbed the bottle of moisturizing body lotion and creamed his skin before he got dressed.

Picking up his cell phone, he scrolled through to review his missed calls. To his surprise, the caller hadn't been Ivy, but his brother.

Marc Damon stood six feet, two inches tall with the same dark chocolate brown coloring as his baby brother. Marc was Jonathan's partner, and also chef at Magic Moments. He and Jonathan shared a special bond. Their mother Ruth died of cancer, and their father died eight months later. They went to live with their aunt and uncle, but promised that they would always been there for each other. He'd have to call his brother later.

Jonathan checked his profile in the mirror before he grabbed his jacket, wallet and keys and headed for the door.

Jonathan pulled up to Ivy's condo with mixed emotions. He hoped his coming over wouldn't make Ivy have a flashback to that dark place that she seemed to have overcome.

Quickly dismissing that theory, he reminded himself that getting to know her was important. What did she do when she wasn't working? What was her favorite color? What kind of movies did she like? Did she like butter on her toast? He wanted to wine and dine her, but he needed that information first.

In his eyes, tonight he would start a journey of discovery. He hoped in the end they would live happily ever after.

❧

Ivy was plain worn out from all her responsibilities the last couple of weeks. She had no idea that winning a contest would garner so much attention. She was grateful that business was picking up, but the show hadn't started yet and her life already showed signs of chaos. Thank God her siblings did their part in their business or she would really be in trouble.

Last night, she laid aside the information on the couples she'd be working with on the show at about two in the morning, when sleep finally claimed her.

For the second night in a row she'd attempted to pull an all-nighter.

Ivy didn't mind working with Jonathan. In the past, when her back was against the wall with a wedding, he allowed her to pitch her ideas to him; if she missed something he'd usually find it.

After her meeting with Jonathan and Lauren, Ivy had gone back to the office to get an update from her receptionist.

She was relieved when Gwen told her that they had the phone calls under control. She'd followed her suggestion of splitting the calls up based on need. If they had generalized questions, Gwen answered them or transferred the caller to Ivy's voicemail.

There were six messages on her voicemail and Gwen had schedule three people to come in to meet with Ivy for next week. New clients made her happy, but she didn't want to sacrifice quantity for quality.

After she got home, she took a leisurely shower and then laid down for a nap. Once she got up, she felt refreshed and ready to work.

She pulled out Lauren's green folder and started reading from the first page. Ivy wondered if the woman truly expected to have everything she listed be a part of her wedding or if they were just wishes.

Glancing at the list of ideas for the ceremony, dresses, invitations, decorations, reception, favors and cake, Ivy knew it all couldn't be done in three weeks. Most of it didn't even go together.

Ivy was certain that she and Jonathan could come up with a cohesive and spectacular alternate plan that would please Lauren just as much.

Ivy slipped on a pair of navy blue slacks and white pullover sweater. She liked walking barefoot in the house, so she didn't bother to put on any shoes. As she slipped her diamond studs in her ears, she heard the doorbell.

She walked to the door, quickly smoothed out the wrinkles in her pants, and looked through the peep hole to make sure it was Jonathan.

She opened the door and stepped aside so that he could enter. He was carrying several large brown paper bags. She removed one of them from him arms to relieve him.

"Something smells good in here," she said, sniffing the bag as she walked through the great room to the large eat-in kitchen.

"I had no clue the kind of take-out you like, so I hope you eat Chinese." He placed the bag on the granite countertop.

"Sure, I like Chinese food." Ivy reached inside the cabinet to retrieve a couple of plates. She sat them next to the food.

"I thought we'd work in the kitchen since it's the biggest table I have. We can work better if we can spread things out."

"Aren't you hungry?" Jonathan asked, removing the cartons of crab rangoons, shrimp egg foo young, shrimp fried rice, beef and broccoli and shrimp with garlic sauce from the paper bag.

"I'm starving. It's been so busy today, I don't think I even ate lunch." Ivy retrieved two large table spoons from the drawer and handed one to him.

Jonathan spooned a generous amount of shrimp fried rice onto his plate. "I was over at Marc and Rose's last night and she told me business has been hectic with all the phone calls and clients coming in for appointments."

"When I entered that contest, I did so because I wanted the world to see how good I was at wedding planning," she said as she opened the lid on the carton of beef and broccoli. Licking the brown gravy from her finger, she continued. "I never thought people would be contacting us so quickly. We haven't even taped the first episode and the phones are going crazy. I just want to make sure we keep things in perspective and don't move too fast. Trying to accommodate everyone and losing the quality of work we've been known for isn't an option for me. That's our staying power." She put a little of everything on her plate and went to the table with it.

Jonathan followed her. "I totally agree. People can tear you down faster than they can praise you."

Ivy had disassembled Lauren's portfolio and had placed the information in two sections. One was for the ceremony and the other was for the reception. In all there were twenty-three pages.

She picked up a page and glanced at the food choices she requested for her reception. "I think you should take a look," she suggested to Jonathan, handing him the white sheet of paper.

Jonathan studied the lengthy list. "I see she wants appletinis as her signature drink." He continued to scan the list. "This is a lot of food. She has three peppercorn strip loin, braised smoked beef brisket, smoked salmon, grilled salmon, the list goes on and on."

"We should suggest doing food stations instead of a sit-down dinner. The guests can choose from all these dif-. ferent entrees."

"That's exactly what I was thinking."

He handed it back to Ivy. "Can you make a copy of it so that I can go over it with Marc? He can better determine what foods and side dishes compliment each other."

"Sure, I can make a copy on my three-in-one printer before you leave."

Ivy pushed her plate aside and reached for another stack of paper.

Jonathan moved his dish in front of him.

"No, you go ahead and finish your meal. I don't want to get too full because if I do then I'll be lazy and not want to work. My bed will be calling my name."

"Understood, but you did enjoy it?"

"Sure, I love crab rangoons and shrimp egg foo young. I just can't eat a lot of it."

Ivy flipped through the papers and scanned the words. "Jonathan?"

He looked up at her. "Yes, Ivy."

"Let me read the list for the ceremony. First of all I think we're going to have to be careful with those lime green and peach colors. We want to create a romantic atmosphere, and if the colors clash it can be a disaster."

A string quartet, DJ, live singers for the ceremony under the gazebo covered with hundreds of hydrangea, calla lilies, and roses. Hand tied bouquets for the attendant's Biedermeier bouquet with apricot calla lilies, jade roses and cymbidium orchids for her bouquet."

"It's too cold to have the ceremony in the garden outside," Jonathan said.

"Let me talk to Rosie about creating something with that same effect. I'm going to go over this with my sisters in the morning. I wanted us to come up with two different wedding day scenarios she could choose from."

"Ah, aren't I special," Jonathan said, placing his hand against his chest. "See, I told you we worked well together."

Try as she might, Ivy couldn't hold in her laughter watching him be silly.

The sparkly and expressive look in her eyes when she worked got him all excited right along with her. He moved his chair closer to hers. "I'm listening."

Suddenly aware of his nearness, Ivy scooted her chair over a few inches, lowering her head groaning in frustration. It didn't work, for her body betrayed her. She could still feel the heat that radiated from him. That heat caused her to want to move closer to it. Working with him on many other occasions had never made her feel the way she felt at that moment.

Maybe because she'd always thrown herself into her work, she never paid attention to how physically close their bodies were in the past. Tonight was different.

She slowly lifted her head only to meet the twinkle in his rich brown eyes. As if her eyes had a mind of their own, they wandered to his luscious mouth. She couldn't deny the fact that she was drawn to him. But what would she do about it?

There was a long moment of silence before Jonathan said, "Go ahead, I'm listening to you."

Mesmerized by the husky sound of his smooth, baritone voice, Ivy hadn't realized that he'd pulled her chair back to him. Uneasiness crept in, and Ivy was alarmed at how prickly she was beginning to feel and how angry her body made her for wanting to be close to him.

She'd better get back to work and get him out of her condo as fast as she could.

It was close to midnight when Jonathan left Ivy's place. He enjoyed watching her face light up as they finally came up with solid ideas for the impromptu wedding.

Pleased and relieved that she was comfortable being so close to him made him want to be around her even more. He wanted to ask her to give him a chance, but he'd have to settle for their date Friday.

By the time he left, they had two partial proposals; one with a sit-down dinner and the other with buffet stations. He needed Marc to make a recommendation for the food and get a quote for the charger plates, linens, chair covers and special glassware, while Ivy discussed the flowers, cake and dresses with her sisters. It looked like they would meet their deadline.

Jonathan wondered if Ivy realized that they had been married for a month now.

CHAPTER 6

A satisfied smile grew on Ivy's face after meeting with the first couple of her show. She had successfully presented her plans for their summer 2011 wedding.

Chiropractors Adrianne Reynolds and Robert Conway met at a Chicago Cubs baseball game three years ago. After they'd dated for eight months, Robert asked Adrianne to marry him with the help of the jumbotron at Wrigley Field.

The young professionals were to marry in a Christian ceremony at the Salem Baptist Church's House of Hope, where the bride was a member. The posh reception, with seven-course meal, would be held at Stanley Hall inside the Field Museum.

Ivy happily answered all their questions and now that both parties were comfortable with each other, they would begin taping in another week. Ivy gave the couple a brief hug before they departed.

As soon as Ivy entered her office, she shrugged out of her coat and hung it on the brass coat rack in the corner.

The spacious and sophisticatedly decorated office had an old antique desk and two white Regency cane-back chairs. She also had dark cherry wood floor-to-ceiling book cases that were filled with reference books on any subject regarding wedding planning and décor. Across the room she had a seating area with a burgundy chenille-covered sofa and two more armchairs.

She kicked off her black high-heeled pumps, lay back against the fluffy pillow on the couch and rested her eyes. It was only ten o'clock, but she wanted to take this small window of down time to relax. She had a long day ahead of her.

Ivy had been up since five o'clock working on both the TV couple and Lauren Kabins's wedding plans. She was confident that all the plans for Adrianne and Robert would be fine, but there were still some pieces missing in Lauren's proposal due today.

She had thirty minutes before she had to meet with her sisters concerning those missing pieces.

After her power nap, Ivy got up, walked over to the gold mirror and freshened up her hair and makeup. She walked over to her desk, picked up the folder and headed to the conference room.

Everyone had already arrived when she walked into the room. She wondered if they'd had the opportunity to be creative since she had given them such short notice, phoning them only last night after Jonathan left.

"Let's get this party started," she said, placing her pen and paper on the table before taking her seat.

"Rosie, you first," Ivy said.

Rose pulled up the laptop computer that was hooked up to a big-screen plasma television on the wall. She opened the file folder where she saved the sketches.

"Because the wedding and reception is in one place, we'll have to set the scene from the beginning."

She turned to Ivy. "Vee, I know you said she really likes tall centerpieces. I do, too, but they can restrict the guests from being able to see the ceremony depending on where they are seated at the table."

Ivy agreed. "That's true. Can you come up with something spectacular that you think she would love?"

Rose opened the first sketch file. "Here is an example of a tall, trumpet-style vase with peach and green hydrangeas, peach and white French tulips."

She then opened the second one, moving the image beside the first one for comparison. "Here is the smaller centerpiece using a round container with the same flowers arranged differently."

Ivy bit the end of her pen as she studied the images. "What about the ceremony? Did you get a chance to come up with something for it?"

Rose went to another file folder and opened a different image. "Do you guys remember what we were going to do for the Hawkins wedding at the mayor's mansion?"

The others all looked up at the screen and nodded. "Well, I think we should do something similar, on a smaller scale, of course. We'll need a focal point, a place similar to an altar. Arches are kind of out of style, but we could create something dramatic with the flowers, fabric and some columns."

"We only have three weeks, Rosie," Ivy warned.

"I know, I know. Don't worry," Rose replied.

"How soon can you have a sample of both center-pieces ready?"

"I already started on the tall one this morning, so I'd say this afternoon or tomorrow morning."

"Good." She then turned to Violet. "Have all the bridesmaids been contacted?"

"I contacted all the girls from the information you gave to me. They came in and I've measured and ordered all three of the dresses. They're scheduled to arrive next week."

Ivy made a notation by the bulleted item for dresses in her notebook. "Is that going to push you for alterations?"

"Only if the young ladies gain or lose too much weight. Otherwise we should be fine. From the three dresses Lauren chose, they really liked the peach lamour satin Bill Levkoff dress, and they run true to size. I shouldn't have to do anything more than a bottom hem."

"What about the bride? Did you get her dress ordered as well?"

"Yes." Violet's eyes lit up. "I must say I was happy to work with her."

"Lauren is a delightful young woman who knows what she wants," Ivy commented.

Rose handed Violet the wireless mouse, and she quickly pulled up the folder with pictures of the dresses. "She chose this beautiful champagne-colored Monique

Lhuillier gown from the ready-to-wear collection. It's due to arrive next week as well."

Ivy beamed. "What a lovely dress. She's tiny, so she'll look fabulous in this flowing chiffon gown."

"I thought so, too," Violet added.

The last-minute wedding was coming together better than Ivy ever expected it to.

She removed two magazine pages from Lauren's folder and handed them to Lili. "Ms. Lili, here is the picture of the cake I was trying to describe to you last night."

When Ivy called Lili the night before to get a head start on the sketches for the wedding cake, she didn't have a description of the cake in the magazine, so she described it the best way she could.

"Were you okay with the description I gave you last night of the cake?"

Lili picked up the magazine page and studied it. "It's a little different from this photo, but I came up with two ideas for the groom's cake and two for the wedding cake from what you told me."

Lili gave her presentation. "Since Lauren said that her fiancé loved to golf, I thought I'd make a groom's cake that looked like a golf bag. The other would be a full sheet cake covered in fondant decorated like a tennis court since you said they like to play tennis. I'll have two figurines; one would look like her and one to look like him."

"Ah, how cute," Violet said.

"I think she'll love the idea." Ivy scribbled some notes.

Lili changed the images. "Now, here are the two images for the wedding cake. The first one would be a three-layered almond torte cake filled with raspberry cream and tri-berry compote covered with fondant. I'll use unrefined sugar crystals to embellish it."

"Sounds fancy," Rose commented.

Ivy nodded. "Okay, very simple and elegant."

"Right." Lili pointed to the next picture. "And this one is seven-tiered tiramisu cake covered with fondant, hand-formed sugar roses and hydrangea florets accented with sugar diamonds."

"This is probably the one she's going to choose. It's very close to that photo," Ivy said, and pointed to the torn magazine page.

"I'm going to set up a taste testing as soon as she decides."

"I've just pulled four from the oven before the meeting; banana, vanilla, lemon and chocolate. They're cooling now. I'm going to use them for the brides that are coming in this afternoon."

"It probably won't be until next Monday. I'll check the schedule after we've gotten an answer."

"This is the fastest wedding we've ever done," Rose commented.

"Ladies, thank you for moving so quickly. I still need to talk to Jonathan about the menu and table linens and such, but I think we're good here."

Ivy adjourned the meeting and went back to her office. She pulled up her e-mail and saw that Jonathan had sent two.

Ivy loved modern technology. Since their office went green a couple of years ago, they've been able to save time by using the computer for their proposals, sketches and wedding project management. Being able to communicate with brides as well as vendors in a split second via e-mail or text had been a blessing to their business.

Now that the proposals were complete, she got them ready to e-mail to Lauren. Ivy then printed a hard copy of all the documents and added them to the rest of her folder. All she had left to do was send them to Lauren and wait.

Lauren called thirty minutes later. Ivy had to hold the phone from her ear so that Lauren's scream of excitement wouldn't burst her eardrum.

She wanted to come in right away with her fiancée to sign the contract; they had decided on one of the two proposals Ivy had sent to her. Ivy gave her an afternoon appointment and now was waiting for them to show up.

Ivy heard the buzz of the intercom. She pressed the button on the phone. "Yes, Gwen."

"Ms. Kabins is here."

"I'll be right down," Ivy said as she stood. She hung up the phone and walked down the hall to the front of the building, where she spotted Lauren chit-chatting with Gwen.

"Good afternoon, Lauren. You look radiant," Ivy commented.

Lauren threw herself in Ivy's arms, surprising her to say the least. "Thank you so much. I'm so excited about my wedding."

Ivy patted Lauren on the back as she hugged her. "You are so welcome, sweetheart."

Releasing her, Ivy stepped back and watched the tears form in the young woman's eyes. "I didn't think I had enough time to have a wedding like this, but you are going to make my dreams come true." Lauren's voice trailed off.

Ivy patted her back and smiled. Lauren's reaction was one of the reasons she loved her job. Once she let go they walked side by side from the front of the building to the back to her office.

"Violet showed me your dress this morning. I love Monique Lhuillier's gowns. They are so classy, elegant and . . ."

"Expensive," Lauren chimed in. "But I don't mind paying when I get what I want."

"That's a good attitude to have, because there are some folks that wouldn't pay $3,500 for a gown that they will only be in for five hours at the most," Ivy said as they arrived in front of her office.

Ivy looked back down the hallway. "I thought your fiancée came with you."

"He's in the parking lot taking a business call. He should be in shortly."

Ivy extended her hand so that Lauren could enter the office first. "Come on in and have a seat. I just need to call Gwen." She offered Lauren one of the empty seats in front of her desk before picking up the phone to call the receptionist.

"Gwen, send Lauren's fiancé down when he comes in. We're going to get started."

"I sure will," Gwen said.

Ivy placed the receiver on the cradle, sat down and opened Lauren's folder.

"Ms. Hart, I don't know how to thank you for helping me."

"No need to thank me, my dear. I love making wedding dreams come true. I think it's why I breathe."

Lauren was talking a mile a minute. Ivy didn't mind, though, because she loved to see people happy and seriously in love . . . something she hadn't thought about in a long time.

The last man she gave her heart to didn't know what to do with it. She promised herself not to risk that kind of love ever again.

Ivy glanced at her watch, and Lauren's fiancée had yet to show up.

"Lauren, what did you say your fiancé's name was?"

"Randall."

"Maybe we should get going; it doesn't look like Randall is coming in anytime soon."

The first document she picked up was the proposal that Lauren had chosen about floral arrangements for the wedding and reception.

"We can walk over to the floral shop and see the sample bouquets. Rose said that they would be done by this afternoon," Ivy suggested before flipping the page.

"Can we wait for Randall?" Lauren asked.

"Sure, we can wait for him."

As Lauren read the notes under the photographs on the page, she said, "I love both options for the reception, but I want to go with the buffet stations. Having more than three entrée selections is important to me."

"We can set it up nicely." Ivy was pleased Lauren had chosen the buffet, for it gave her more variety and she could get most of the items on her list. She still saved money, even though it was pricier than the family style served meal because she had three kinds of fish, filet mignon and seafood, but Lauren didn't seem to mind the cost.

"Let me call Rose and see if the sample centerpieces are ready now." Ivy picked up the phone and pressed the intercom button to Rose's shop.

"Yes, Vee."

"Are the samples ready? I have Lauren Kabins in my office." Rose created breathtaking floral designs, and Ivy was excited to see her sketch in person.

"I'm almost done. Give me about twenty minutes and I'll bring it to you."

"Okay," Ivy said before disconnecting the call.

"Let's go ahead to choose the invitation and I can have those in the mail by Monday." Ivy got up from her desk and walked into a room adjacent to her office, pulled a large three-ring bound book filled with samples of wedding stationery from the shelf and brought it back to the office.

"Did you still want to wait for your fiancée?"

Lauren gave a sheepish grin. "Would you mind? I really want him to be part of the planning process."

Ivy placed the book in front of Lauren and checked her watch as she went back to her chair behind the desk. "Don't feel bad if he doesn't come inside, Lauren. Most men don't really get involved in the planning anyway. They are usually satisfied if the bride's happy. I have an idea, if he doesn't show up, he can come to the cake tasting." She pulled up the calendar to check for an opening. "You guys can come next Monday morning at ten o'clock."

At that moment Gwen appeared. "Ivy, Lauren's fiancée is here," she said, stepping back and letting a towering figure come forward.

Ivy gasped.

Stunned, Ivy scrambled to recover from the entirely unexpected sight of Randall Holloway in her office, of all places. She had no idea that when Lauren said her fiancé's name was Randall that it would be the Randall she'd known for years.

A trained professional knew how to handle things like this, but Ivy never thought she'd have to deal with this type of situation. She hadn't imagined seeing him again. She hoped her eyes weren't playing tricks on her. The day had turned into a nightmare.

Smiling brightly, Lauren jumped up and threw her arms around her fiancée. "Baby, what took you so long?"

Randall kissed Lauren on the forehead, but his eyes were on Ivy. "William needed to talk to me about my new job contract."

Taking his hand, Lauren led him over to the other chair in front of Ivy's desk.

"Baby, I'd like you to meet Ivy Hart; she's the woman I told you about."

His face blank, Randall extended his hand. "Hello, Ivy," he said politely.

Ivy stared at the outstretched hand; she couldn't believe his nerve. Not wanting Lauren to think she was rude, she accepted his hand.

"Nice to see you again, Randall," she said, remaining seated.

Lauren looked back and forth between Randall and Ivy. "You two know each other?"

Ivy answered first. "Yes, we went to grad school together."

"Wow, how ironic is that?" Lauren said. "You never told me you knew Ivy."

"I know so many people, I didn't think about it," he said noncommittally.

Also sidestepping Lauren's curiosity, Ivy said, "It's okay, Lauren. Anyway, we've got a lot to do, so since we are all here now, let's pick up where we left off."

CHAPTER 7

Ivy slumped in the chair behind her desk for more than ten minutes after Lauren and Randall left her office. When she closed her eyes, all she saw was Randall. The broad shoulders, chiseled face and close-cut black hair hadn't changed in the ten years since she'd last seen him.

As if seeing him wasn't enough, putting her hand into the strong grip of his massive hands had almost made her want to throw up. But she couldn't allow his presence to affect how she did her job.

Sitting up straight in her chair, she opened the folder with the signed contract, looked over it before picking up the phone to call Jonathan.

"Jonathan Damon."

"Jonathan, how are you today?"

"I'm good, but what's wrong with you? You sound funny." There was a pregnant pause before Jonathan spoke again. "Don't tell me she didn't like the menu Marc suggested."

"She liked the menu and was very excited about everything. She actually chose the proposal with the food stations."

"Great, and she's good with the sides and vegetables, too?"

"She's good," Ivy said, thinking that their client didn't have a problem, but she sure did.

"What time do you want me to pick you up tomorrow?" Jonathan asked, changing the subject.

Ivy frowned; she had no idea what he was talking about. "Pick me up for what?"

"Don't tell me you've forgotten we are supposed to go on a date Friday night."

Ivy smacked herself upside the head. She'd completely forgotten about their date, which now, thinking about it, may not be such a good idea. After the other night and the way that her body betrayed her, she was uncomfortable being around Jonathan.

All she wanted was peace and harmony in her life. The way things were pre-Las Vegas. It wasn't *One Life to Live* or some other soap opera; it was her life, and she wanted to live it peacefully.

Ivy felt bad canceling the date, but she needed to tell him now, so that he wouldn't show up at her place on Friday.

"I don't think we should go out, Jonathan."

Jonathan clenched his jaw. He didn't know how to read Ivy. One minute she was warm and pleasant, and the next she was cold and distant. He wanted her to make up her mind about the date once and for all.

"Oh, so you're trying to back out on me." He didn't want to pressure her, but he wanted her to realize what she was doing.

Ivy sighed deeply. She needed to do something to relax, because coming in contact with Randall made her realize that they had some unresolved issues; she knew in her heart that she would see Randall sooner than later. "I'm just saying, I've got a lot of work to do and I'm already tired."

"I thought we'd settled those issues earlier this week."

"Did we?" Ivy was running out of things to say. "Look, Jonathan, I'm going to be honest with you. I haven't been out on a date in a while. Most time my work consumes me, and I really like it that way. I don't risk my heart being broken."

"I'm not going to hurt you, Ivy," Jonathan said, his voice low and husky.

"We've already started out on an emotional roller coaster after our escapade in Las Vegas," she said.

"I know it was not my best decision, but I want to get to know you and for you to know who I am on the inside." Jonathan blew out a big breath. "Ivy, I'm attracted to you. I think you are beautiful, smart and have something to offer a man. I want to be that man." After a long pause he said, "Now I've got my cards on the table."

Ivy had no idea that calling him would reveal his feelings. She could no longer deny that she was attracted to Jonathan, but she knew from past experience that attraction isn't enough.

"Where do you want to go?" he asked Ivy.

"I don't have a preference, Jonathan. You just let me know if I need to dress up or wear something casual."

"I told you that you would have the time of your life when you went out with me. I want you to dress up, and not like you're going to church, either."

They both chuckled.

Ivy had to admit, Jonathan could always make her laugh.

"Okay, I'll be ready."

The next day, Ivy received a phone call from Sally Carter, the reality show producer. She told her that Adrianne and Robert had broken off their engagement, so they would be shooting the premiere episode with the second couple, Marsha Anderson and Blake Moore. Because of the short timeline, they would messenger their information to her to study for the shoot, which would start at seven o'clock on Monday morning.

Frustrated and amazed at how quickly the television execs switched the couples around like pieces on a checker board, Ivy jotted down as much information as she could pry from Sally in order to get a head start.

She was also saddened when she thought about how Adrianne and Robert must have been feeling. She just knew the two were in love . . . inseparable. Ivy wondered if their being on the show contributed to their ending their engagement. She'd never know.

Being a professional, she would have to roll with the punches.

Trying to put the new turn of events in the back of her mind, she logged on to her computer and opened an e-mail from Lauren. She'd sent the names and addresses of her guests, most of whom lived in the area.

The rest of the plans for Lauren's wedding were going well. She'd agreed to Ivy's idea for the perfect stationery and favors. They'd booked the venue, chosen the linens and the menu and ordered the gowns.

She was about to pick up the phone when it rang.

"Yes, Gwen."

"Randall Holloway is here to see you."

Her intuition never failed her. Ivy knew she'd see Randall again sooner rather than later. The cold look in his eyes the other day told her that they still had unfinished business, and that he'd be back without his bride.

Balancing the phone on her shoulder, Ivy flipped through the appointments. Was it possible that Randall and Lauren had an appointment? She doubted it. He came to see her.

"We don't have an appointment scheduled for Lauren today. But send him down." She didn't need to tell Gwen that she and Randall had a past.

Ivy met Randall her sophomore year of grad school at Michigan State University. She majored in communications and he was an engineering major. They dated through college and grad school. She thought she'd found her soul mate. They wrote out their goals and plans for their future together, but all that changed one Thursday night ten years ago.

Ivy pressed her back against her high-backed antique chair and folded her hands, resting them on the desk. She took a deep breath as she heard his footsteps on the marble floor in the hallway.

His body filled the doorway, and the determined look on his face confirmed Ivy's thoughts that he was angry.

"How can I help you, Mr. Holloway?"

Randall stopped when he was directly in front of her desk.

"After all we meant to each other, I'm just Mr. Holloway now?"

"This is a professional establishment and you are one of my clients. What else do you want me to do?" Ivy replied matter-of-factly.

"Don't act like I'm a stranger."

Ivy leaned forward. "Randall, what do you want? I know you didn't come here to talk about us. You're getting married, remember?"

Randall sighed loudly. "If you hadn't walked out on me, maybe you and I could have been married."

Now furious, Ivy pointed at the door. "Get out of my office. You're marrying Lauren in less than two weeks. I wish you both all the happiness in the world."

But Randall did not leave; instead he walked around to the other side of the desk and confronted Ivy.

"What happened to my baby?" Randall asked angrily.

Ivy stood up, pushing him back and moving to the other side. His nearness was making her feel closed in.

"What are you talking about, Randall?"

"Don't act like you don't know what I'm talking about, Ivy," he blurted, his voice raised.

Ivy rushed to the door and closed it. She didn't want anyone to hear his crazy accusation.

"What the hell do you care?"

"What happened to my baby?" he repeated.

Gazing at the man she had once loved with all her heart, Ivy couldn't believe what she was hearing. He is the one who turned his back on her, and now he had the nerve to come and ask questions.

"Randall, you don't deserve to know."

Now in a rage, Randall pointed his finger at her. "I have a right as that child's father."

Finally, she had had enough. "Shut up, Randall," she said. Her words were deliberate, her tone uncompromising. "Just shut up."

Brushing aside Ivy's demand, he kept talking: "I didn't really want you to get rid of the baby. I was just shocked; a baby at that time wasn't in our plans."

She pointed to a chair. "Sit down and shut up. I have more important things to do with my time than to argue with you about something that didn't happen."

"Are you trying to deny me an explanation as to why you killed my child?"

"I'm not denying you anything, Randall. I'm actually trying to set the record straight."

Collecting her thoughts, Ivy sat in the chair next to him. "See, this is what happened between us that last time. You never listen; you take things and twist them and don't allow the other person to fully explain. Well, today you are going to hear the truth about what really happened the night I came to your apartment."

She waited a moment to see if he was going to interrupt her again.

"Two days before I came to your apartment, I took a pregnancy test. When it came back positive, I didn't know what to do. I couldn't tell anyone, so I kept it to myself, trying to decide how I felt about it."

Randall started to speak, but Ivy held her hand up to silence him.

"Let me finish. In my own way, I had to come to terms with the idea of having a baby. It was not in our plans, but things happen. I thought we loved each other and that love would be enough to love our child. I came over to your apartment that night to tell you. Your first words were 'get rid of it.' "

Leaning forward, Randall made a feeble effort to explain himself. "I didn't mean what I said. I was just caught off guard, surprised."

"I think you have selective memory. You never said you were surprised, and you sure didn't act like it."

Releasing a frustrated sigh, Randall reached over to touch Ivy's hand.

She snatched her hand away. "Don't touch me, Randall. I need to finish what I have to say. Remember when you tried to stop me from leaving and I slipped?"

"Yeah, I rushed to you, but you refused my help and got up and left. I even ran after you, but you kept moving without looking back."

"I know. I was fine until later on that night. I fell hard down that flight of stairs. My knee was paining and I hurt my elbow from the fall. During the night, my stomach started cramping and I knew I had to get to the hospital right away."

Rising, Ivy went over to the window as the pain of that evening came rushing back. Tears came to her eyes, despite her efforts to keep them back. She'd finally gotten the chance to tell him what happened, but she left out one little detail. She'd gone to her regular doctor as a follow-up and was told that she had a weak uterus and would have possibly lost the baby anyway without medical intervention.

Randall came over and stood behind her. Gingerly, he began massaging her shoulders.

"Please don't tell Lauren about what happened between us."

Ivy jerked away from him, moving swiftly to her desk. "Do you think I could be that indiscreet, that insensitive, that unprofessional?"

She picked up the files on her desk and began shuffling them aimlessly, finally adding, "I think you should find another coordinator. This isn't going to work."

Not waiting for a response, she dismissed him by picking up the phone and pressing a button.

"We're done here."

CHAPTER 8

There was something wrong and Jonathan knew it as soon as he walked into Ivy's condo Friday night. The energy in the room had dwindled from his last meeting three nights ago. It was quiet and Ivy seemed sad, but not the sad that he saw in her face the day she summoned him over to her house. Even then there was plenty of fire, but tonight it was as if someone threw water on the burning flame.

As soon as she opened the door, she offered him a seat and disappeared down the hall without another word.

He wanted to go after her, to hold her, to caress her, to make her feel better, to take away the hurt he saw in her eyes.

"Is everything okay?" he yelled.

"Yes," she shouted back.

Jonathan didn't believe her. He'd been around her long enough now to know that her mood had changed from yesterday.

As Jonathan waited for Ivy, he looked around the living room and admired the décor. Directly off the entry, the room was both open and intimate, as well as being immaculate.

She'd chosen contemporary furnishing in deep brown colors. The warm camo-green walls and eggshell-colored trim created a great backdrop for the large pieces of art-work that hung on the wall.

Not wanting to wait any longer, he stood to his feet and walked toward the hallway, so he wouldn't have to yell, but she appeared before he could get any closer.

"Wow, you look fantastic." He couldn't believe Ivy had let her hair down. He really liked the loose, wavy curls that framed her face. It made her look sexy. Right then, he could imagine running his fingers through it.

"You did all this for me?" he commented, hoping to get her to smile.

Ivy turned her eyes upward and swatted at his arm. She blushed, which made Jonathan's heart smile. He didn't want to see her upset.

Picking up her hand, he twirled her around so he could get a better look at her outfit. "Every man in the restaurant is going to be envious of me."

"Jonathan, you are so crazy."

"No, I'm serious," he said pulling her to his chest. The top of her head met his chin. He bent down and kissed her hair.

Ivy looked up and met his intense gaze. They stayed that way for several moments.

"Needed a hug?" he asked her.

When she remained silent, Jonathan slowly pulled her closer to him; if she wanted to resist, he'd let her go. Moments later, he could hear her exhale.

When he released her, Jonathan stepped back and lifted her face with his hands so that he could see her eyes. "Whatever's going on, it's going to be okay."

Ivy only nodded, turned and walked away.

Jonathan watched her as she went over to the coat closet. He still admired the way her black two-piece pants suit fit her body. The cut of the double-breasted jacket hugged her breasts and the notched lapel collar revealed the sensual neckline of her creamy, coffee-colored skin. The jacket had a bias cut peplum in back with three-quarter-inch bell sleeves. She wore black high-heeled boots.

Ivy opened the door and removed her gray wool swing coat. "Where are we going, anyway?"

Jonathan went to help her with her coat. "I thought we'd go to Andy's Jazz Club in Chicago."

Ivy smiled at him. She thought his gentle gestures were kind, and she never knew the power of a hug. Walking into his arms felt so good; his strong arms around her made her feel safe. As soon as her breasts touched his chest, she released all of the tension she'd held inside. Nothing had ever felt that good. She appreciated him for trying to make her feel better without prying.

Ivy was glad they weren't going anyplace around town. She didn't want to run into Randall. When she left East Lansing to come back to Taylor, he was still there. Growing up in Detroit, she wondered how Randall ended up in Taylor, but she was thankful that they hadn't run into each other before yesterday. She didn't want any part of him.

Taking her black leather coat from the hanger, she handed it to Jonathan. "I've never been there before. Do you go often?" She slipped into it while he held it for her.

"I've been a couple of times, but not lately. I go there when I want to show a beautiful woman a good time," Jonathan said as he watched Ivy pick up her hand bag.

He followed her out of the door and out to his vehicle.

Jonathan opened the passenger side door and helped her up into his black Range Rover. Closing the door, he trotted around to the other side and climbed inside, started the truck and they were on their way.

Glancing at Ivy from time to time, Jonathan noticed she'd gotten quiet again. Suddenly, it came to him that maybe someone in her family had found out about their marriage.

"Ivy, can I ask you a question?" He glanced over at her, then looked back at the road.

"Sure, what is it?" Ivy turned her body in his direction.

"Did someone find out about us?"

"Oh, no," she said, and then paused before saying, "Unless you told."

Jonathan reached over and gently picked up her hand. "No, I didn't. I promised you that I wouldn't. I only asked because you seemed upset, so I thought one of your sisters found out."

"No, it's nothing like that," she responded, then turned away looking out the passenger side window into the night sky.

They road silently, until Jonathan pressed the button on the console and the smooth sounds of Will Downing filled the air.

The words of the song seemed to soothe her, and he saw her lean back and relax. Seeing her this way made him want to fix things, to reassure her, but not with words. He took a chance and reached over, picking up her hand and firmly squeezing it for reassurance.

"What was that for?" Ivy looked over at him. She knew all too well that he was trying to be a friend.

"I know there is something bothering you. I understand if you don't want to share it with me, but know that I'm here for you if you want to talk."

Suddenly, out of nowhere, tears sprung up in her eyes. She didn't dare blink because they would surely spill down her cheek, so she looked the other way until she composed herself.

Then turning back to him, she said, "That's sweet, Jonathan, but I'm fine. Really."

Jonathan took his eyes off the road momentarily to look at her. "Okay, good. I don't want people to think I'm a bad date." He chuckled, hoping she would laugh with him, but she didn't.

"Babe, can you get three dollars out of the cup holder for the toll ahead?" he asked as he approached the Chicago Skyway. He really didn't need her to get the money, for he always kept it in the cup holder so he could access it easily. He wanted to keep her interacting with him.

Ivy adjusted herself in her seat, reached down between them and retrieved three one-dollar bills. She handed them to him.

"Thanks."

"Jonathan, tell me about Andy's. What kind of food do they serve?"

"It's not a real fancy place, but they have great appetizers, salad, sandwiches, pasta, pizza, steaks, ribs and chicken. The food's pretty good, but I think the music is off the hook."

"Is that why you chose this place for us?"

"Yes, I thought we'd have a little candlelight, food, conversation and music. Just a relaxing evening since neither one of us have to work tomorrow."

Ivy sighed. "It feels good not to have to get up early in the morning. But the show's producers are sending me information on a new couple for the taping on Monday."

"What happened to the other couple you were studying?"

"I was told that they canceled their engagement, so they couldn't be a part of the show. Remember, it is reality TV, so the couples had to be getting married for real."

"Wow, that's too bad."

"It really is. When I met them, they looked like the sweetest couple. I thought they were happy. Now, I'll be taping the first episode with new people."

"Well, we're going to relax and have a great time tonight. You can worry about the new couple on Monday."

Jonathan eased off the expressway at the Stony Island exit ramp and followed it to Lake Shore Drive.

As she stared out the window, Ivy was fascinated by the beauty of Lake Michigan; even in the wintertime, it was beautiful.

They drove silently for several more minutes until Jonathan found a place to park down the street from the club.

Coming around on the passenger side, he opened the door and assisted her down out of the vehicle. Jonathan shut the door, hit the locks, and reached for her hand.

Ivy looked at his outstretched hand and, without hesitation, grabbed hold of it.

Jonathan clasped his fingers with hers, pulling her gloved hand to his lips and placing a light kiss there.

They stayed that way, walking to the building side by side. Jonathan smiled at her as he opened the door to the entrance of the club. Walking past him, Ivy returned his smile and waited for him to follow her.

For the first time that evening, Jonathan felt hope.

CHAPTER 9

Jonathan asked the waiter to seat them so they could still see the stage, but have some privacy. He was pleased with the corner table toward the back.

Keeping the conversation light, Jonathan suggested a pasta dish for Ivy to try as they scanned the menu. Jonathan watched the other couples on the dance floor, swaying to the music.

Laying the menu aside, he rose from his seat and extended his hand to her. "Let's dance."

At first, Ivy stared at him. Dancing with Jonathan would mean being close to him. Her breast against his chest, the feel of his arms around her, the warmth and that feeling of wanting to get closer made her heartbeat accelerate.

"I won't let anything happen to you, baby. I promise. Remember we came here to relax and have a good time."

Ivy threw caution to the wind even though her mind screamed that she shouldn't. She caught hold of his hand, rose to her feet and followed him to the dance floor.

Jonathan gently pulled her into his solid chest. Ivy's body melted as he drew her closer.

Just as she thought, the intoxicating scent of his woodsy cologne drew her even closer to him. When his lips grazed her ear, she relaxed and laid her head against his chest, her left hand splayed across it, allowing herself to get lost in the rhythm of the music.

The band that was on stage was one she'd never heard before. They played contemporary jazz, but reminded her of the group Incognito. The soothing sound of the piano and saxophone mixed with the powerful tone of the vocalist magnified Jonathan's touches.

Jonathan lifted his head and when she did the same, he stared into her eyes. His eyes were mesmerizing and she didn't want to be anywhere else but right there in his arms.

Ivy rested against his chest, but squeezed him tighter when he whispered in her ear, "You are so beautiful."

Soon the song ended and he gently caught her right hand and led her back to the table.

"I see you are enjoying the music. I really like this band," Jonathan said as he pulled out Ivy's chair.

"I love the woman's voice. It was so soothing," she said as she took her seat.

Jonathan went to the other side of the table, then looked at her. "You know what?"

"What?"

"You are too far away from me. I have to reach across the table to touch you. I need to be close to you, and this table is in the way."

"Well come over here, then," she said and patted the empty seat next to her.

She was captivated by Jonathan's tenderness, manners and affection toward her. He really was a sweet guy.

Jonathan looked pleased by her response. Moving swiftly to the other side of the table, he pulled her into his arms. "Now, this is better."

Looking down at her, he smiled and said, "Isn't this better for you?"

Ivy giggled. She moved slightly out of the circle of his embrace and thought about him seriously. He was warm, funny, kind and professional, and she was glad she had a chance to see his sensitive and considerate side.

She had to be honest with herself. She had only been angry with Jonathan for a short time. He never pressured her and kept their secret. She still had several months before it would be too late for an annulment. Jonathan was nothing like Randall.

As soon as the thought of him popped into her mind, the anger and sadness returned. Then she thought there still was the issue of Randall. Her gut was telling her that he was going to remind her every chance he got not to tell his fiancée about their past together.

"What is it, baby?" Jonathan rubbed her shoulders slowly, noticing her distraction.

Ivy inhaled deeply in an attempt to pull her emotions together. She moved out of his embrace. "I'm sorry, Jonathan."

Rubbing her hair to try to soothe her, he cradled her chin between his thumb and forefinger. When their eyes met, he said, "Whatever it is, you can tell me."

Scanning the room, he noticed that the other couples weren't paying any attention to them.

Ivy laid her head on his shoulder. Jonathan wrapped his arms around her and held her until she had a chance to relieve herself of whatever was plaguing her.

A short blonde-haired young woman came over to the table. "Would you like something to drink?"

Jonathan looked over at Ivy, waiting for her response before he gave his order.

"I'll have a glass of white wine," she said confidently.

"I'll have the same," Jonathan added.

"Are you ready to order?" the waitress asked.

Jonathan shook his head. "Give us a few minutes, please."

The waitress walked away and Jonathan used his right thumb to remove a tear that had slid down her face.

"What happened? I thought you were having a good time."

"You are so sweet, Jonathan," she said and touched her face with her palm. "I haven't been out on a date in a long time. The music and the atmosphere are just right."

"Well, what's the matter, then?"

Ivy wiped her face. "Nothing's wrong. I just thought about something."

Jonathan didn't believe her. He wanted Ivy to trust him, to tell him how she was feeling, so that he could help her. "I can't sit here and see that you're hurt and not do anything. You said earlier that whatever you were upset about had nothing to do with us, so I need to know if someone is trying to hurt you or has hurt you."

He hoped she could hear the sincerity in his words. He cared about Ivy and never wanted any harm to come to her.

"Look, Ivy, your husband is supposed to be your best friend, confidant. You should feel comfortable enough to share anything with me . . . good or bad."

Husband? Legally, he was, but that was not at all what Ivy wanted. She wanted so badly to relieve herself of the thoughts and feelings she'd had since Randall showed up at her office yesterday. Why not Jonathan? He's already carrying one secret, she thought to herself.

Ivy was too embarrassed to tell her sisters. They had no idea that she was ever pregnant, and she didn't want them to know how careless and irresponsible she'd been.

Jonathan gently stroked her back. "Are you ready to tell me?" he asked.

"It's about my new client," she said, moving away from him slightly.

Jonathan's face was a mask of confusion. "Ivy, I can't believe that you're allowing that young couple's breakup to get under your skin to this extent."

Ivy moved slightly away from him. "It's not just any client. It's a little more complicated than that."

"Okay, tell me what's so complicated about it."

"The groom used to be my boyfriend," she said cautiously, waiting for his reaction.

Jonathan threw his head back and laughed. "What? Are you upset that he's marrying another woman?"

Her eyebrows furrowed. "No."

He immediately regretted his question. "I'm sorry, Ivy, I didn't mean to sound so insensitive."

She stared silently, trying to figure out if he was trying to cheer her up or if he was making fun of her.

Jonathan lifted Ivy's right hand. "Seriously, I'm sorry, baby, for asking that question. Go on and tell me the rest."

"The guy is Lauren Kabins' fiancé."

Jonathan's eyes widened. "Really? Didn't you know that this fellow . . ." He snapped his fingers. "What's his name?"

"Randall."

"Yeah, Randall. Didn't you know that he was Lauren's fiancé when you met her?"

"We were moving so quickly with the wedding plans, that I only asked her his name yesterday," Ivy said.

The waitress came back. "Are we ready to order, sir?"

"You know what? I don't think we are going to order anything right now. If we decide, I'll call for you."

The waitress nodded and left them.

Jonathan turned back to Ivy. "Let me get this straight. You dated Randall, who is Lauren Kabins' man."

Ivy nodded.

"Is that why you were so upset? He showed up at your place marrying someone else?"

Ivy punched him in the arm. "No, no, no. He came back this morning accusing me of something that I didn't do . . . I'd never do."

Jonathan sprang to his feet.

"What are you doing?" Ivy wanted to know why he was getting up.

Grabbing his coat, he said, "I think we should go someplace a little more private to discuss this." He retrieved his wallet and, removing several bills, tossed them on the table.

He picked up her coat and assisted her into it when she stood.

Wrapping his arm around her, he whispered in her ear, "Do you want to go back to your place or mine?"

Ivy frowned at him.

"We would only go there to talk. I just think you need to tell me in private."

Buttoning her coat, she said, "We can go to your place."

CHAPTER 10

Both Ivy and Jonathan were quiet on the drive back to Taylor. He wondered what was going through Ivy's head. Whatever she was going to tell him about Randall, it must have been something awful to make her so sad.

When Jonathan pulled up to his apartment, he turned off the motor and turned in his seat toward Ivy.

"Are you ready to go inside?"

"I really think I'll feel better once I get this off my chest," she said, unbuckling her seat belt.

Jonathan came around and opened the door for her. She followed him into the building and to the elevator.

Once they were inside his apartment, Jonathan helped her out of her coat. He pulled off his coat and hung them both in the closet.

Taking her elbow, he guided her into the great room. "Take off your shoes and relax. Let's get comfortable so we can talk." Jonathan walked toward the kitchen. "Would you like something to drink? Water, tea, wine?"

Ivy took a seat on the leather sofa. "No, I don't want anything right now."

Jonathan came back and sat down beside her. He didn't sit very close to her because he wanted her to know that he truly was interested in what she had to say.

"Okay, now, finish telling me about Randall coming to see you."

Ivy clasped her hands in her lap, but she didn't say anything. She didn't really know where to start.

"Well . . . well, I was pregnant . . . once."

A cloud of confusion covered Jonathan's face. He was silent for a moment and then he moved closer to Ivy.

"Pregnant? By whom, Randall?"

Ivy nodded.

Jonathan couldn't believe what he was hearing. "What happened to the baby?" So many thoughts swirled in his head.

"Randall wanted me to get rid of it, but I miscarried." Tears welled up in her eyes.

"That son of a . . ." Jonathan stopped himself before he'd gone too far. Randall had a lot of nerve asking her to do something like that.

"When he came into my office today, he actually accused me of getting rid of it."

"He didn't know that you'd miscarried?" Jonathan asked.

"The day I had the miscarriage, I'd gone to see him to tell him about the baby. He lived on the second floor of a three flat building not too far from the university we both were attending. When I told him I was pregnant, Randall was furious. He went on and on, saying hurtful things like how could I do this to him, this was not in the plan and he didn't want to be a father right now, so I rushed out of the apartment. He ran after me, pulling at my coat. I yanked it back and fell down the stairs." Her tears flowed freely.

Jonathan shook his head trying to process everything she was telling him. "Wait a minute, Randall didn't go with you to the hospital? Where was he?"

"He did try to help me, but I got up, ran to my car and sped away. I didn't know that there was something wrong until after I'd gotten home. He didn't know I went to the hospital."

Jonathan moved closer, their knees touching. "So, did he call or come over to your place so you guys could talk?"

"Yes, but I didn't answer my phone. I didn't want to keep hearing his reasons for my getting rid of my child."

Jonathan pulled Ivy into his arms. "I don't blame you."

Ivy pulled away. Now that she started explaining, she wanted to tell him all of it. "I woke up in the middle of the night with severe cramps. I knew there was something wrong. I was only eight weeks pregnant."

Jonathan couldn't believe what he was hearing. "Did you call Randall? How did you get to the hospital?"

"I didn't want anything more to do with Randall, so I drove myself. I'll never forget the sterile smell of that emergency room or that bald-headed doctor telling me that I had had an early miscarriage."

Jonathan reached over and squeezed her hand as a gesture of comfort. "Were you upset that you'd lost the baby?"

Ivy got up and walked across the room and stood in front of the entertainment system. "Honestly, I was all over the place. At first I felt relieved, being a twenty-four year old; I didn't want to bring shame upon myself and my family, so that's why my sisters don't know about it. Then I felt guilty about losing the child.

I went to *my* doctor a couple of days later because I wanted to find out if what the emergency room doctor had told me was true. Did I lose it because of the fall down the stairs or what? People fall down the stairs all the time and don't lose their babies." She paused.

"In the end Randall got what he wanted, I just never told him."

Jonathan went to her. "I don't blame you. He was an insensitive bastard." He hugged her.

Ivy stepped back. "When he came to see my today, with all those silly accusations after all this time, I just looked at him like he was crazy."

"Is this the first time you've seen him since the night of your fall?"

Ivy nodded. "Yep. It's been ten years. Can you believe that he asked me not to tell Lauren?"

Jonathan wasn't surprised at Randall's behavior, and if Ivy was honest with herself she wouldn't be either. They were harboring a secret, too. Even though it didn't involve a child, it did affect their lives.

"I can believe it. He probably thought that you were still angry with him and that you'd tell his fiancée about his past in order to shatter his future."

Ivy threw her hands down. "When I left Michigan, I left all thought of him behind. I will be so happy when we get him married off. If I don't ever see him again, it will be too soon."

Jonathan reached out and pulled her into his arms and held her. "I don't ever want you to go through that kind of hell alone again," he said before kissing her forehead and leading her back to the sofa.

"When is the next time you're scheduled to see him?"

"At the cake tasting next Monday morning at ten."

"I thought you said that you had that taping."

"I do. That's this Monday, but we're shooting the segment on the couple at my office for our consultation."

"Well I'm going to be there next Monday for the cake tasting, too."

Ivy rested her hand on his. "You don't have to do that, Jonathan. I don't think he'll say anything with Lauren there."

He lifted her hand up. "Doesn't matter," he said. "I know we have our issue with the marriage and all, but right now you're my wife and I'm not going to allow him to mistreat you."

Ivy was overwhelmed by Jonathan's words. He was sensitive to her needs and a great listener. "Thank you so much for listening to my problems." She scooted closer and gave him a hug.

Surprised but pleased by her actions, Jonathan wanted to continue his date. This conversation was the start of one of the most important elements in a relationship: trust. Ivy proved that she trusted him.

"Are you hungry?" he asked.

"I could eat a little something," Ivy replied.

Jonathan stood up and said, "Good, because I'm starving." He walked over to the kitchen area, opened the drawer and pulled out several take-out menus.

Holding them up, he said, "Pizza, Chinese, fish, chicken. Take your pick."

Ivy jumped up and walked over to him. "You don't have anything here we can cook?"

Thinking quickly, Jonathan opened the refrigerator. Since he only ate at home on occasion, it was mostly empty.

"The only food in my refrigerator is a package of boneless chicken breasts, a head of lettuce and a package of bologna that I picked up last week."

Ivy chuckled and shook her head. "Where are your seasonings?"

Jonathan stared at her as if he didn't know what she was talking about.

"Jonathan, do you mean to tell me that you don't have any salt and pepper?"

He smiled. "Yes, I have that, but I don't have all those fancy seasonings like my brother uses. The only reason I have the chicken breast is because a lady was giving away samples in the store. It was good, so I bought it."

"I understand. So where is the salt and pepper?"

He opened the cabinet next to the stove and pulled out the package of chicken breasts and a head of lettuce. "We can whip up a grilled chicken salad in no time," she said.

Jonathan stood right next to her watching as she methodically gathered what she needed for the quickie meal.

Ivy looked over at him. "You really don't cook?"

"I do get sick of going out to eat or over to a family member's house, so I tried several times."

"How did it turn out?"

"I threw it in the garbage."

Ivy looked puzzled. "Why did you throw it away? Didn't you eat some of it?"

"No, the steak was rubbery and the chicken I tried to fry wasn't done. And so you don't want me to cook tonight, there's no telling how it will come out."

They both burst into laughter.

"Maybe you should leave the cooking to me, then. I don't want either one of us to end up in the hospital with food poisoning."

Jonathan was elated. "Sure, whatever you say." He went over to the cabinet where the pots and pans were kept. "Which skillet do you need? I know I can do that right."

"Do you have one with the grooves? Remember, we're going to grill the meat," she said, rinsing off the chicken breasts. "You can wash and cut up the lettuce."

Saluting, Jonathan said, "Aye, aye."

Working together this way emboldened Jonathan. He walked behind her. "I keep telling you we are good together."

Ivy could feel the heat from his body. She leaned back against his chest, her eyes closed.

Jonathan gently pushed back a wisp of hair covering her ear. "Ivy, don't fight us, just give us a chance," he said, his voice now raggedy and hoarse.

What he wanted to do was to make love to her right there in the kitchen. On the table, the counter, the floor, it didn't matter. He just wanted to be inside her, but he knew she wasn't ready. At least she was starting to trust him.

Releasing her, he walked over to the fridge and got an unopened bottle of white zinfandel. He then got two wine goblets from the cabinet over the sink and went to the table to wait for her.

"Jonathan, do you have any music by that group we heard tonight?" Ivy asked, plating their meal. She placed the dishes on the table just as he got up from his seat.

"No, I don't but I do have some other jazz," he said, going over to the entertainment system. He picked up his iPod, which was hooked up to his sound system. He chose the playlist from the small device, and the next thing they heard was Peter White playing his acoustic guitar.

Jonathan went back to the kitchen and poured himself a glass of wine. He raised the bottle in her direction. "Would you like me to pour some for you?"

"Yes, I'll have half a glass. It's getting late and I still have some reading to do when I get back home."

Jonathan poured the golden liquid into the round glass. "I thought you were going to relax this evening," he said as he handed her the glass.

"I'm relaxing with you now. And I must say I'm having a great time."

Jonathan gave her a warm smile before digging in to his meal. "This is good. It's too bad I can't boil water."

"Jonathan, a bachelor needs to know how to feed himself."

With his eyes tilted up, he said, "Technically, I'm not a bachelor." He couldn't resist; the words just rolled off his tongue.

Ivy ignored his remark and asked a question instead. "How's business for you guys?" She changed the subject on purpose because that was a heavy subject for her.

"Business is good. We booked three wedding receptions and a corporate Christmas party today."

Ivy smiled. "I'm glad the business is a success for you and Marc," she said, picking up her wineglass.

"Are you nervous about the show?" he asked.

Ivy looked up from her plate, careful not to look into his eyes. That's what really made her nervous. Every time she did so, she would see the passion, kindness and concern in them. If she looked into the depths of his brown eyes, she would surely end up in his bed tonight. She'd better hurry and finish dinner so he could take her home.

CHAPTER 11

Jonathan pulled up in front of Ivy's condo, released his seatbelt and turned to her. "I had a good time with you tonight, Ivy."

"I really enjoyed the evening, too, even though I ended up cooking."

They both laughed.

Ivy released her seat belt and leaned over, intending to give Jonathan a kiss on the jaw. Instead the kiss landed on his full lips.

Realizing what had happened, Ivy broke the kiss and looked away.

"Ivy, I enjoy being around you. Even when you are trying to play hard or be serious, I just enjoy your company. And now that I've proven to you that we're good together, I would like to spend more time with you." He caressed her cheek.

Ivy knew she had to make a decision about Jonathan. He'd done nothing since they came back from Vegas but try to support and please her. Deep down, she wanted to spend more time with him.

"I want to spend more time with you, too, Jonathan," she finally admitted.

Jonathan jumped out of the vehicle, ran around to the passenger side. Opening the door quickly, he assisted her down and escorted her to the front door.

Jonathan glanced at his watch. "It's getting pretty late and I think we've had an eventful evening," Jonathan said, leaning against the side of the door.

Ivy chuckled. "You mean the drama I dropped on you. Yeah, you handled that well." She pulled her keys from her purse and placed it in the lock.

"Don't you worry about Randall. I'll take care of him."

Turning the knob on the door, Ivy pushed it open and stepped inside with Jonathan right behind her.

"I don't want you to cause any trouble, Jonathan."

He raised his right hand and crossed his heart with his left. "I won't, if he won't."

Jonathan stepped closer to Ivy. "I have a question for you, though."

Before Ivy could find out the question, Jonathan captured her face in his hands and tasted her sweet lips. He retreated.

He returned again, pulling her closer, and Ivy was lost in his kiss. She moaned and he followed, deepening the kiss, causing his hands to move from the expanse of her back to caress her behind. His manhood stretched with her body pressed against him.

When he finally released her, he rested his forehead against hers, whispering hoarsely, "I needed that."

Taking two steps back, he stared at her with passion-filled eyes. "Goodnight, baby," he said before turning around and walking out the door.

Ivy stood silently at the door watching him leave. Her body was alive, passion coursing through it. For the first time since she and Jonathan got married, she believed she was ready for a relationship . . . one with him in it.

On the way home, Jonathan thought about his encounter with Ivy. He willed to constrain himself from going too far with her. That first kiss left him wanting more, but once he tasted her lips the second time, he all but devoured her. She was as warm and responsive as he hoped she would be.

Replaying his conversation with her, she revealed the number one reason why she had trust issues. They were very well deserved. He was grateful that she trusted him enough to tell him her secret. And he understood her reasons why he couldn't tell her sisters. Now that all that had been revealed, he wanted her to heal, to move on and live a rich life. Preferably with him, but even if they didn't work out, he wanted her to have her heart's desire.

Next Monday, he would be present to see for himself how Randall acted. He hoped for Randall's sake that he did his business and left. He parked his car and went into the house, and all his thoughts were on loving Ivy.

CHAPTER 12

Ivy got through the weekend reading the bios and other information about Marsha and Blake, so she was fully prepared when they arrived for the television shoot.

Before she left home, she called her sisters to remind them that they were wearing their royal blue Hearts and Flowers uniforms for the shoot today instead of their regular clothes.

She liked the ensemble, which consisted of black slacks and a royal blue button-down cotton shirt with the company crest embroidered in white and gold on the left breast pocket.

Ivy stopped by Lili's office to tell her that Randall would be stopping in with his fiancée just in case Lili recognized him.

When she walked in all three of her sisters were sitting in the work room laughing.

Ivy walked into the room. "What's going on, ladies?"

Rose got up and walked over to her. "Good morning, Ms. Superstar."

Ivy waved her hands. "Girl, please," she responded, before walking over to Lili.

"I'm glad all of you are here. There's something I need to tell you."

Lili, Violet and Rose gave her their full attention. "Remember that guy I dated when I was living in Michigan?"

"Uh-huh," Rose mumbled.

"Ronny, Raymond, or something like that," Lili guessed.

Violet sat up straight. "Nope, his name was Randall." She looked at Ivy for confirmation. "Right, Vee? Wasn't that his name?"

"Yes, Randall. Anyway, he's marrying Lauren Kabins."

Lili pushed Ivy's shoulder. "Girl, if you don't get out of here with that mess."

"You are kidding right, Vee?" Rose asked.

"No, I'm not. I just wanted you guys to know in case he comes for the cake tasting with her."

"Isn't he like forty or something, and she's a toddler," Lili joked.

"He's marrying her, that's all I can tell you," Ivy said, not wanting to get into any personal speculation about his relationship with Lauren.

"How do you feel about it?" Violet asked.

"I feel fine. We haven't been in touch with each other in more than ten years." Ivy moved toward the door.

"I needed to tell you that, so there would be no confusion." She looked at Lili. "And don't you start anything with them, either."

Lili laid her hand over her chest. "Me? I wouldn't do that."

They all burst into laughter.

Ivy pointed at her. "I mean it. We don't need another incident like the one we had with Dianne Hawkins and her fake-Gucci-wearing daughter Phoebe."

Rose stood to her feet. "Oh, Vee, they deserved everything they got."

Ivy concluded that she had to make sure that she was present for the cake tasting because the last time she let her sisters handle a hostile customer they had to call security. Even though she knew the customer made the incident personal, she couldn't afford anything like that getting out on her now.

"I'm going up front so that I can see if Marsha and Blake have shown up yet. The film crew should be setting up any minute now."

Lili glanced at Rose and Violet. "How's she gonna come in here, drop a bomb like that and then leave? Oh, no, sistah girl, this conversation ain't over."

The television taping went well. Ivy really enjoyed working with Marsha and Blake. Marsha had the most intriguing greenish gray eyes. The tall, ebony colored young woman sporting a short, spiked haircut towered over her fiancé, Blake, who had to be about five feet, seven inches tall. The two were professionals; she worked as a mortgage broker for a neighborhood bank and Blake was a high school music teacher.

They were high school sweethearts, and then went their separate ways when Blake went off to college. They reunited a year ago when he came into the bank after accepting a job at Wyndam High School.

A fun-loving couple with great tastes, agreed to the plans Ivy had made for them. They'd chosen to have their ceremony and reception at one venue, the top floor of the Chicago Hilton and Towers on Ninety-fifth Street in Chicago.

With the help of a very understanding film crew, the taping of the show was a breeze. They would tape two more times this week, and that footage would be edited and combined for the first episode. Ivy looked forward to next week.

Later that afternoon, Rose walked into Ivy's office and sat down in the chair in front of her desk.

"We're going ice skating on Saturday, wanna come?"

"I think I'll pass. I don't skate, remember?"

"It will be a lot of fun. You should come. Jonathan is coming with us."

"And . . ." Ivy knew Rose was trying to play matchmaker. "Did you talk to Jonathan about this before you tried to set him up on a date?"

Rose blushed. She held up her hands in surrender. "Okay, Vee, you got me. Marc is going to talk to Jonathan about coming along. I just think you'll like him, if you get to know him."

"Rosie, I just went on a date with him last Friday."

Rose scooted closer to the desk. "Yeah, and you didn't even tell us how it went."

Ivy pushed her paperwork aside and clasped her hands together, trying to figure out what she should say to Rose without revealing her true connection to Jonathan.

"Okay, if he agrees to go, then I'll go."

Rose got up and smiled. "Good. I'll see you tonight, then."

After her sister left, Ivy couldn't deny the fact that even though she'd spoken to Jonathan on the phone several times since their date, she was eager to see him again.

In fact, she had relived every sensuous moment of their date; every sweet kiss, every touch and every gentle caress. This was the kind of man that had only shown up in her dreams.

Gwen buzzed in, bringing Ivy back from her day-dream. Ivy pushed the button. "Yes, Gwen."

"Jonathan is here to see you."

"Thank you," Ivy said before hitting the button.

She quickly went to the wall mirror to examine her hair and makeup. She smoothed out her clothes and waited for him to come in.

"Hey, baby," he said as he walked into the office.

A shiver went down Ivy's spine at the sight of his towering figure and the sound of his raspy voice.

"Hey." Ivy liked the term of endearment. "Rosie just left my office. She wants me to go ice skating Saturday."

"Yeah, I know. Marc and I just talked about it."

There was a pregnant pause before Ivy spoke. "Is that why you came over here?"

"Yes, and I needed something else, too."

Ivy didn't remember how or when he pulled her into his arms, but suddenly she found her breasts pressed against his chest, sending waves of passion coursing through her body.

The next thing she knew, Jonathan's lips were on hers, and Ivy became instantly lost in his kiss. When she moaned, his hands went from her shoulders to her waist, deepening the kiss as he brought her even closer.

When they came up for air, Jonathan whispered, "I needed that."

Ivy blushed, but met his gaze. "What do you think about going skating this Saturday?" After that kiss, she could barely string a sentence together.

"I think it will be fun."

Ivy hadn't been skating since she was in high school. "Jonathan, I don't know how to skate."

"That's not what Rosie told me."

"She talks too much," Ivy said and smiled.

"Don't be afraid. Rosie and Marc, Destiny and Nicholas, Vanessa and Richard and my friend Kenny and his wife Monica are going, too."

Jonathan once again kissed her lips. "I'll be there to catch you if you fall," he said, trying to reassure her.

"This is going to be interesting," she said, smiling at him. "Where are we supposed to meet Rosie?"

"Marc wants to drive us, so I'll be at your place by seven. We'll drop my truck off at their house."

Jonathan beckoned for her with his index finger. Ivy closed the gap between them.

"Just one more kiss and I'm out of here."

"One more."

He leaned forward and surrounded with his arms, resting his head against her. "I'll see you later."

Ivy kissed him back. "Okay, see you later."

Jonathan walked out of the office and Ivy sat at her desk, reveling in the unexpected direction her life was going.

CHAPTER 13

Saturday evening, Jonathan arrived at Ivy's house at six o'clock. He decided to come early so that they would have time to spend together before they had to go to Marc and Rose's house.

Ivy opened the door and said, "Be careful where you step, my contact lens just fell on the floor."

Jonathan raised his foot to check the bottom of his shoes and tip-toed around her, as he looked down at the carpeted floor. "Where were you when it fell?"

With her left hand, Ivy made a circular motion in the area to the right of where Jonathan was standing.

They both got down on their knees and gently ran their hands over the carpet in that area, trying to find the missing lens.

Jonathan spotted the clear round disc. "Baby, I think I've found it." Carefully he lifted it from the floor with his forefinger. Holding it up, he gave it to her. "Don't these things tear or dissolve?"

Ivy carefully took it from him. "Yes, I have to be so careful. Thanks so much. I thought I was going to have to buy some new ones."

"Don't I get some kind of reward or something for finding your precious lens?" Jonathan gave her a big smile.

Ivy couldn't help but laugh at him. "Give me just one minute." She ran to the bathroom and poured saline solution on the lens and gently rubbed it to clean and moisten it.

She placed it in her eye and when she looked up, Jonathan had stuck his head inside the bathroom door.

"I'm still waiting on my reward."

Ivy turned to him and kissed his cheek.

"Is that all I get? Girl, you kissed me like I was your Uncle Bubba."

Ivy playfully hit his arm. "Let's get ready to go."

Jonathan blocked the doorway to the bathroom. "Nope, not until I get a proper kiss."

Ivy playfully placed her hands on her hips. She knew he was kidding around with her, and she actually liked it.

Walking over to him, Ivy pulled him to her and kissed his forehead, his nose and then his lips.

Breaking the kiss, she stepped back. "Better?"

"Better," he said, grabbing her hand, pulling her out of the bathroom and down the hall.

Glancing at his wrist, he checked the time. "We'd better get going. I don't want to start anything we can't finish."

It had been a year and it still surprised Jonathan how in love Marc and Rose were. He never thought a woman would be able to capture his playboy brother's heart until he met Rose. The sweet and nurturing dark-skinned beauty was just what his brother needed.

He pulled up to the Victorian-style house and turned to Ivy. "You ready?"

She nodded.

He got out and walked around to open the door for her.

Walking up the sidewalk together, Ivy rang the door-bell.

Marc answered the door. "Baby, they're here, hurry up," he yelled toward the stairs.

"I'm coming," Rose yelled back.

As the brothers embraced, Marc asked, "Did Aunt Rachel call you?"

"No, why? Is something wrong?" Jonathan asked.

"No, she wants us to help her with the canning this year."

"With all the females in our family?" Jonathan asked, recognizing one of his aunt's ploys.

"Who knows? But I'm going to be there, and I think you should, too," Marc replied, checking the time and looking toward the stairs. "Baby, come on," he called out.

"I'll go and get her," Ivy said, heading toward the staircase.

Ivy looked for Rose in her dressing room, but she wasn't there. She then walked down the hall toward the bathroom. She could hear sounds, but wasn't sure where they were coming from. The closer she got to the bath-room door, the louder the sounds became.

Once she was directly in front of the door, she real-ized her sister was crying. It broke Ivy's heart. Rapping on the door, she called out, "Rosie, it's me. Open the door."

"I'll be out in a minute," Rose responded.

"No, I want to come in."

Ivy stood in front of the closed door for what seemed like an eternity. When the door flew open, she walked in and gathered Rose into her arms. "What's the matter, Rosie?" she asked, stroking her sister's hair.

"Vee, I don't know what's wrong with me," Rose said, dabbing her face with a tissue.

Ivy led her over to the tub and they sat facing each other. "What do you mean? Are you sick?"

"No, I'm not, but there's got to be something wrong with me," Rose replied, her voice small and sad.

"Rosie, I'm not following you. Can you start from the beginning? Why do you think something is wrong?"

"We've been married for two years and I haven't gotten pregnant yet."

Ivy searched for words to ease her sister's pain. "You will; stop worrying. I bet you'll get pregnant if you don't think so much about it."

"I've tried to push it to the back of my mind, but I just can't. I want to be a mother so badly."

Ivy felt her stomach tightening. She hadn't even thought about whether or not she could be a mother her-self after what happened to her. She couldn't allow her feelings to show too much, though. Rose had enough going on, and she didn't need to add to her concerns.

"Why are you going skating, then? Aren't you afraid that you might fall down?" She didn't want to be the voice of gloom, but her sister had to be realistic about things.

"I'm not going to skate; I'm just going to be with you guys." Rose gave her a half smile.

Ivy hugged her sister to her, saying, "Let's get your face cleaned up." They both stood and went to the mirror over the basin.

Studying her sister's reflection in the mirror, Ivy said, "Stop feeling sad. I think you'll be a wonderful mother. We've got to get downstairs before your husband comes looking for you."

As they headed for the door, Rose stopped and said to Ivy, "I really hope you like Jonathan, Vee, he is such a nice guy."

Ivy thought to herself, but didn't say it aloud. *I know and I think I'm in love with him.*

When they walked into the kitchen, Jonathan was on one cordless phone and Marc was on another.

"They must be talking to Rachel," Rose guessed.

The men quickly ended their call.

"Is Rachel all right, baby?" Rose asked Marc as she moved into his arms.

Marc kissed her forehead and said, "She's fine, ready to do her canning. She wants us to help her with some other stuff around the house. She doesn't want Uncle Isaiah on the ladder, and he's too cheap to pay somebody else to do the work."

"So M & J to the rescue," Jonathan joked. "Hey, we'd better get out of here; Vanessa is probably driving Richard crazy by now," he added as they headed out the door.

CHAPTER 14

Ivy hadn't had so much fun in a long time, at times feeling like a teenager. At first she had refused to go on the ice, but Jonathan kept telling her it was like riding a bike. She finally relented when everyone insisted that she join them.

Ivy had trouble keeping her balance, and Jonathan's assistance didn't help much. He held her hand or wrapped his arms around her waist, and his sheer nearness was disconcerting, making it hard to even keep her balance. She had finally gotten the hang of it, and ended up being happy she had gone out with him.

After going to a fast-food restaurant, they headed home.

Leaning back against the headrest, Ivy closed her eyes and reveled in the fact that she was completely relaxed.

"Tired, baby?"

"Yes, but a good tired." Ivy smiled, but kept her eyes closed.

Jonathan parked his vehicle in front of her house and eased his arm around her shoulder, drawing her closer. After kissing her passionately, he said, "I had fun, too. We've definitely got to do this again."

"Do you want to come inside?" she asked, her face flushed from the kiss they just shared.

Jonathan looked intently at her. "Are you sure?"

Ivy nodded before saying, "Yes."

They got out of the car and went inside.

"Have a seat. I'm going to change into something more comfortable," Ivy said, leaving him in the room.

Leaning back against the sofa, he rested his arms on the back of it and said, "Make it something sexy."

Ivy admitted to herself as she walked down the hallway to her bedroom that she didn't know what she was doing, but she was going to roll with it because tonight was the night.

Trying to figure out what to wear wasn't easy. She loved pretty, silky lingerie, and had an armoire full of it, but had no idea what he liked. She rummaged through her drawer at first, then suddenly had a devious thought. "Jonathan, can you come here for a minute?"

Jonathan got up from the couch and walked down the hall. "Where are you?"

"I'm back here," she yelled.

Once at the door, he saw her standing in front of her dresser wearing a short navy blue silk robe.

"Can you help me find something you would like?" Ivy asked innocently with a peach and black negligee hanging from the tip of her finger and a lacy blue thong dangling from the other.

Jonathan clenched his teeth to keep from running across the room to grab her. "You don't have to wear anything."

Ivy dropped the lingerie back in the drawer and said, "As you wish."

Without thinking about what she was doing, she loosened the tie around her waist, causing the robe to come apart and revealing her blue lacy bra and panties.

Jonathan moved farther into the room, meeting her. Ivy fingered the collar of his black polo shirt before kissing him lightly on the lips.

"Girl, you better stop playing with me," he said, attempting to restrain himself from picking her up and taking her over to the bed.

"What did I do?" Ivy asked innocently.

"Don't play innocent little schoolgirl with me, Ivy."

Ivy wrapped her arms around his neck and rubbed the back of his neck.

"So you want to play, huh?" he whispered huskily.

Ivy kissed his neck in response.

The atmosphere in the room changed dramatically. There was no more kidding around; this was serious.

Jonathan stepped back and looked into her eyes. "Are you sure? I don't want you to hate me in the morning."

Ivy's stomach tightened and she took one step forward. "I'm sure," she whispered in his ear, then nibbled it with her teeth.

Excitement exploded in every nerve of his body as he slipped her robe off and watched it fall gently to the floor.

Reaching around her, he unhooked her bra in one smooth motion. Pulling the flimsy material forward, he paused to give her time to move away in case she was having second thoughts. When she didn't move, he finished removing it and pulled her to him.

"Ivy, you are a beautiful woman," he whispered, dipping his head and lightly kissing her right nipple first, then the left.

Ivy was grateful he was holding her; otherwise she would have surely hit the floor.

Jonathan reached up and massaged her temple before undoing her pinned-up hair. Running his fingers through her loose curls, he said, "You look so sexy with your hair loose and free. I want that for you like nothing else."

"What?" she asked, trying to focus because she was a bundle of nerves.

"To be sexually free; no inhibitions."

"Show me," she said, her hand moving to his belt buckle.

Jonathan lifted Ivy into his arms with ease and carried her over to the bed. He gently lay her down on top of the covers. He kicked his shoes off and climbed into the bed beside her.

For a few moments, he just drank her body with his eyes, from the beautiful wisps of dark-brown hair that had fallen in her face to her perky dark-brown nipples and her flat stomach.

Jonathan kissed the tip of her nipple again, almost sending Ivy over the edge with anticipation of what was to come.

He rained small kisses on the surface of her stomach before moving further down her body. The warmth of his lips on her skin made Ivy feel as if she was going to come off the bed.

Jonathan peeled back the top of her panties and kissed the exposed skin. Ivy panted as she helped him push the lacy material over her butt and hips and down her legs.

Shaking his head, Jonathan said, "It doesn't make any sense for a woman to have a body like yours."

He got up, reached in his wallet and retrieved the small gold foil packet; he then pushed his jeans and underwear to the floor and stepped out of them, releasing his manhood.

Watching him, Ivy's tongue was stuck to the roof of her mouth; she wanted to say something but couldn't. She marveled at the fact that he was about to make love to her.

Jonathan got back into the bed on his haunches, rolled the condom on to his rigid sex, and positioned himself between her thighs. He gently grasped her legs and pulled her down to him. Seeing the fear in her eyes, he stopped suddenly.

Rising on his knees, he caressed her face.

"What is it, baby? Don't be afraid," he said, trying to reassure her.

Jonathan moved next to her and gathered her into his arms. Maybe he was moving a little too fast. He was anxious to make love to her again, and maybe he had scared her when he'd pulled her toward him.

Moving several loose strands of hair from her face, he asked, "Did I scare you just now?"

"No, I'm fine," Ivy lied. Besides that fateful night in Las Vegas, when she was impaired by alcohol, she hadn't been with a man since Randall.

"We don't have to go any further if you don't want to," he said, reassuring her that even though he wanted to make love to her like there was no tomorrow, he would stop.

Ivy pushed Jonathan on his back and lay her upper body across his. The intensity of her need shocked her, so she could only imagine what it did for him.

As Jonathan caressed her buttocks, their lips met, releasing all their pent-up desires. He pulled her fully on top of him so she could feel his desire.

With his hands firmly palming her behind, in slow motion, Jonathan moved her body up and down against his. Watching the anticipation on her face, he knew it was time to move to the next level.

Lifting her, he quickly positioned her beneath him. With a deep kiss, he parted her legs and touched her wet heat; she was ready, and he was glad. He needed to be buried deep inside her, her long legs wrapped around his waist.

Ivy didn't think she could stand anymore. When he touched her feminine core, that was her undoing. If he didn't make love to her, something bad was bound to happen.

Jonathan positioned himself at the entrance of her heat, pushing gently. Suddenly, Ivy pushed her body forward, bringing him deeper inside her.

Feeling her tight, wet heat wrapped around his engorged sex, Jonathan moved slowly, but methodically, causing them both to gasp at the delicious sensations the motions created.

Ivy caught on to the rhythm and moved with him. Her heart beating next to his felt as if their heartbeats had become one.

Jonathan started to slow the pace.

"Don't stop," Ivy pleaded, caressing his face. She climbed higher and higher with every stroke. They could hold back no longer. Suddenly their pleasure rushed forth, spiraling them to ecstasy.

Ivy had never experienced this feeling. She felt wonderful and free. They lay next to each other, breathing deeply, thinking about where they had just gone as they drifted to sleep.

CHAPTER 15

Ivy snuggled closer to Jonathan's warm body. She could feel him kissing her forehead, nose and neck. Then he wrapped his legs around hers.

Slowly, she opened her eyes.

"Good morning, sunshine," he said. A smile touched his lips as he stared at her, his head propped up on his right hand.

He leaned forward, kissing her lightly on the lips. "How are you feeling this morning?"

Ivy stretched luxuriously. "Happier than I've been in a long time."

Jonathan kissed her bare shoulder. "I'm glad I had something to do with that."

She ran her hand across his chest. "Me, too."

His demanding mouth descended upon hers, moving closer to her until their lips touched.

After he ended the kiss, he rested his forehead against hers. "You know I'm crazy about you, Ivy," he said, his voice soft and low. After an awkward moment of silence, he said, "You don't have to say anything."

Ivy rapidly blinked her eyes. She wanted to respond, but didn't know what to say; his words had taken her by surprise. But there was no doubt she loved him because she'd given him her body, something she didn't take lightly. So her actions confirmed her feelings; she just wasn't ready to say the words.

Instead she said, "I'm still trying to take it all in."

He caressed her face. "I understand." Releasing her, he threw back the cover and sat up on the side of the bed.

Looking back at her, he asked, "Why don't we go out for breakfast?"

Pulling the sheet up over her, Ivy replied, "Good idea, but by the time we get dressed it will be too late for breakfast and too early for lunch."

"We can go to Tiebels. They serve brunch on Sundays." Jonathan stood. "Do you mind if I take my shower first?"

"There are plenty of towels in the little closet in the bathroom. Help yourself."

Ivy watched how his dark chocolate skin glistened in the light of the early morning sun as he walked out of the room.

Momentarily closing her eyes, Ivy lay in bed, her arm thrown over her face, reflecting on how unbelievably fantastic her experience with him had been the night before.

The memory of the heat from his body pressed against hers, the way his mouth caressed the tender places of her body, only fueled the fire inside of her, making her want him more. Their lovemaking was like nothing she'd ever experienced before.

"Ivy," Jonathan called out to her, breaking into her thoughts.

Ivy got up, slipped on her robe and went to the bathroom.

"Yes, Jonathan? You need something else?"

"I need you to wash my back."

"Wash your back?" she repeated.

Jonathan turned around, looking over his shoulder. "Yeah, there's a spot I can't reach," he said, giving her an example.

Ivy shook her head and said, "I've never washed a man's back."

A wide smile grew on his face as he noticed her free flowing hair and dark nipples through the sheer robe.

Moving the shower head to the side, he turned toward her. "There's a first time for everything." He opened the shower door and handed her the soapy white wash cloth.

Ivy tried to tear her eyes away, but she couldn't. Her pulse raced and her body tingled at the sight of him; he was magnificently built.

Taking the towel from him, she washed his back in an up and down motion from the outside of the shower, watching as the soapy water ran down his back and disappeared into the crease of his tight behind.

"That feels good, baby."

"Good."

Jonathan turned around, his eyes twinkling with desire. "Now, the front."

Ivy rubbed his chest first in a circular pattern. Jonathan covered her hand, moving the towel down to his shaft, which was erect.

With trembling hands, she gently caressed his manhood with the towel; all the while every sensitive nerve in her body came alive.

The heat rose in Jonathan's soulful brown eyes. The only thing on his mind was his lengthening sex and the beautiful woman in front of him . . . his wife.

"Now you know if you come in here, you're going to get your hair wet."

Ivy could see the desire in his eyes, and she was ready to join him. Loosening the knot of her robe, she slipped it off, letting it hit the floor.

Stepping forward, she whispered, "That's okay. It will be worth it."

Jonathan immediately slipped his arms around her waist when she joined him, pulling her against his hard body.

With Ivy's arms wrapped around his neck, he stopped the water flow and guided her to the back of the shower, where he sat on the granite bench and pulled her onto his lap. He kissed her lightly on the lips and gazed into her dark-brown eyes.

Ivy rested her forehead on his. Dropping her lids, she proclaimed, "I love you."

Both stunned and touched, Jonathan continued studying her before confessing, "I love you, too." Sealing his statement, he kissed her wildly.

Jonathan stopped abruptly. "This isn't going to work," he said, lifting her up from his lap and standing.

Reaching outside the shower door, he pulled a large bath sheet from the wall rack. He wrapped Ivy in the navy blue bath sheet and swooped her up into his arms. "When I make love to you, I want us to be in the bed."

Holding on to him tightly, Ivy did not protest.

Jonathan walked down the hall into the bedroom, closing the door with his foot.

A short time later, the doorbell sounded.

"Baby, I think there's someone at the door," Jonathan said after hearing the chime of the bell.

Ivy glanced at the clock on her night stand to check the time. They had fallen back to sleep and it was now nine-thirty. She never had any friends come over on Sunday morning, so it had to be one of her sisters.

The doorbell sounded again.

Maybe if I don't answer, they'll think I'm not home. She snuggled closer to Jonathan.

"Babe, my car is sitting outside," he reminded her.

Ivy snapped her fingers. "Dang, I forgot about that."

The doorbell rang again.

Ivy got up from the bed. "I better answer. It doesn't look like they're going to let up."

"I'll be here when you get back," he said.

Ivy walked over to the dresser and pulled out a night-shirt, slipping it over her head as she walked out the room.

Standing on the tips of her toes, she looked through the peep hole. She took two steps back and said, "Damn, it's Lili."

Lili probably recognized Jonathan's car outside. She would ask a million questions, Ivy thought.

"Yes," Ivy said, watching Lili reach out to press the button again.

"Vee, open up," Lili yelled from the other side.

Ivy opened the door and Lili stepped inside.

"Is that Jonathan's truck outside?" Lili asked.

"What are you doing over here this time of morning on a Sunday?" Ivy asked her, pulling the collar of her gown together.

Lili stared at Ivy. "Remember, you told me to come over here on my way to church to pick up the clothes you were donating to the battered women's shelter."

"Battered women's shelter?"

Lili frowned, and then started looking around the room. "Yeah, you said you didn't think you were going to make it to church on Sundays until your schedule let up, so you asked me to come and get the stuff."

"Baby, where's the lotion?" Jonathan interrupted. He came around the corner with only a towel to cover his body.

Ivy jerked her head in his direction. She turned back and saw the shocked expression on Lili's face.

She decided there would be no need in trying to explain Jonathan's presence, so she wouldn't.

"Oh, hey, Lili," Jonathan said.

"Mornin," Lili said, her eyes on her sister.

"Well, well, well," she said, stepping toward the front door, "I see you're a little busy, so I'm going to get going."

"Don't you want the clothes?" Ivy asked her.

Lili waved her hand forward. "Naw, I'll get them another time. I'll let you get back to *whatever* you were doing."

She removed the paper she'd held underneath her arm, handing it to Ivy. "Oh, yeah, I checked out your column in this morning's paper. Great job!" She winked at Ivy, opened the door and rushed out.

When she left so fast, Ivy knew what was coming next. She ran down the hallway to the bedroom, where Jonathan was putting his clothes on.

"How much do you want to bet that Walter Cronkite is going to go blabbing to Violet and Rosie?"

"Walter Cronkite?"

"Yeah, that's what we call Lili. She tells everything she knows or thinks she knows. Plus she's nosey, so she's going to try to pull the other two in to get the info."

Jonathan chuckled. "Family," he said, buttoning his shirt.

"Watch, my phone is going to ring."

Ivy started a countdown, five, four, three, two and before she could say one, the phone rang.

"Vee?"

"Good morning, Rosie," Ivy said, and then mouthed the words *told you* to Jonathan.

Nobody said a word.

"Girl, Lili just called us and said that Jonathan was at your house," Violet finally said, breaking the silence.

"I didn't believe her," Rose said.

"He is here, Rosie," Ivy admitted.

"In a bath towel," Rose stated.

"You have such a big mouth, Lili," Ivy said. There was no answer, so she continued.

"I know you're on here. I think you set a record, it wasn't even ten minutes this time."

"I told you guys he was there," Lili said. triumphantly.

"Don't hurt yourself, girl," Rose said.

"Ladies, I've got to go, I'll talk to you later," Ivy said before hanging up. She lay back on the bed and burst into laughter.

"You'd better get dressed," Jonathan said before he heard the buzzing of his cell phone.

He picked it up from the nightstand and looked at the caller ID. He glanced over at Ivy. "Guess who?"

"Marc, I bet." Ivy shook her head. Their siblings were acting like middle school children.

"What up?" he said after pressing the talk button.

"You tell me," his brother said.

"We'll talk about it later, okay." Jonathan hung up, ending the call.

Ivy was still sitting on the bed. "What are we going to do about them?"

She picked up the newspaper, turned the pages so she could find her article.

Jonathan slid his belt through the loops. "Nothing, we're going to finish getting dressed, go eat and leave our siblings to their shenanigans."

He came around to the other side of the bed and bent down and kissed her softly on the lips. "And you're not going to let your cackling sisters get to you, either. You deserve to have a man in your life."

Ivy stared at him in appreciation for how he handled the situation. Sure, he was sexy and sweet, and now she knew that he was a great lover, but there was much more to him than she'd realized. She admired him for his loyalty, protectiveness and sense of humor. She got up and prepared to go out with her man.

CHAPTER 16

Jonathan pulled into the first free space he could find at the crowded restaurant. Tiebels had been in the area for over fifty years and they were known for their Sunday afternoon brunch. They served bloody marys and Cointreau mimosas, crustless ham and egg tarts, cracked pepper and brown sugar bacon, vanilla challah French toast, and layered fresh fruit salad.

They made their choices and found a table near the window.

"Would you like a bloody mary or a mimosa?" Jonathan asked.

Ivy stared at him.

Jonathan held up his hand in surrender. "Oh, baby, if you don't want it with the alcohol, we can always have them use 7-up instead of champagne in the mimosa."

Ivy stared at him before they both burst into laughter, remembering the time they shared in Vegas.

"Man, that was a crazy time," she said, taking a bite of the delicious bacon.

"Why don't we just have them substitute the champagne for us both," Jonathan suggested.

"We had wine the other night, so I'm okay with it the way it is. It's just for some reason when you said bloody mary, it made me think of Vegas."

Jonathan wanted to ask her feelings about Vegas now that their relationship was on track, but he didn't want to do anything that would trigger a negative response from her.

He looked down at the newspaper she'd brought along with her. "Have you read the article yet?"

Ivy shook her head slowly, pushing it over to him. "No, I'm a little nervous about it. The editor told me that I would write this column for a month and then they would see how well it does before possibly making it a permanent part of the Neighbors section."

Jonathan picked up the paper off the table and opened it. He looked up at her and asked, "Do you want me to read it aloud or what?"

"Lili said it was good, but I'm not ready yet. So you read it and tell me what you think."

From time to time as Jonathan read the article, he'd smile and look up at her.

"What?" Ivy asked, picking up her glass and taking a sip of her champagne and orange juice.

"This is good, baby. You give good advice."

Ivy released a sigh of relief. She didn't know if the column was going to work out with all her other responsibilities. Not wanting to spread herself too thin, she'd decided once she'd turned in her column that if it didn't work out she wouldn't be upset. One woman can't do everything.

Jonathan laid the paper aside and reached for Ivy's hand. "Tomorrow is a big day for you. Are you ready to face Randall again?"

Ivy hadn't thought about Randall in a week. Since she hadn't heard from him since she'd left the office, she figured everything was okay.

"No, I'm not nervous or anything. I hope he just comes and takes care of his business and leaves."

Jonathan turned his head to the side, hunching his shoulders. "Well, doesn't matter what he does, I'm going to be there to see for myself." He squeezed her hand.

Ivy leaned over close to him and placed a wet kiss on his lips. "Thank you," she whispered.

Jonathan's body reacted to the kiss and the sexy sound of her voice. "Girl, don't start nothing in this restaurant." He picked up his glass. "Let's hurry and eat, so we can get back to your place."

They completed their meal and headed back to Ivy's place.

As she was getting out of the car, Ivy suggested, "Why don't we watch one of my favorite movies, *Love Jones* with Larenz Tate and Nia Long? I have it on DVD."

"Sure, as long as I get to spend more time with you, I'm game." He closed the door and followed her inside.

"I'm going to pop some corn and you can put the movie on. It's on the shelf above the DVD Player." Ivy walked into the kitchen. She placed the bag of un-popped corn into the microwave and waited until the bag had expanded. Pouring the contents in a large bowl, she opened the refrigerator and pulled out two bottles of sweet tea, then joined him on the sofa.

Jonathan stretched out and Ivy lay between his legs as they watched the classic film. Midway through the movie, they both fell asleep.

Ivy awakened first. Careful not to wake him, she moved slowly to an upright position. Glancing at the television, she saw the movie had ended.

Carefully studying him, she watched his chest rise and fall, the smooth features of his face and relaxed expression, his full lips, the point on the tip of his nose. The wideness of the palm of his hand as it lay across his chest. She was amazed at the fact that he'd spent the night and most of the day with her.

She reached out to caress his face when he started to wake up.

"Hey, you," he said pulling himself up in an upright position. He looked at the television.

"We must have been tired," Ivy commented.

A smile touched the corners of Jonathan's lips. "Of course, with all the lovemaking we've done in the past twenty-four hours, we have the right to be tired."

Ivy blushed.

Jonathan glanced at his watch and stood up. "I better get going. I need to stop by Aunt Rachel's."

Ivy stood as well. "Okay, call me after, then."

Jonathan bent down and reached for his shoes. "Okay." He sat and slipped his shoes on, then picked up his coat.

Ivy followed him to the door and they shared a passionate kiss before he left.

Once she closed the door, she decided that ,she needed to talk to someone about her feelings. She didn't want to tell Rose because she was married to Jonathan's brother, and she didn't want to share with Lili because she didn't think she could talk to her in confidence. The only person she could talk to was Violet.

Ivy picked up the phone and called her younger sister. "I need to come over."

"I'm here, come on," Violet said.

Ivy got up and put on her shoes and coat, grabbing her purse and keys as she walked out the door.

CHAPTER 17

Jonathan couldn't help but smile as he thought about the blissful two days he'd shared with Ivy. It felt good being with her, sharing a meal, loving her.

He pulled up to his aunt and uncle's ranch-style home and spotted his Aunt Bertha's car.

His aunts had been meeting every Sunday afternoon to quilt together. They'd been making quilts for cancer patients for the last eight years. It all started as a tribute to Jonathan's mother Ruth, who died of breast cancer when he was nine years old.

The quilts had become so popular that they decided to continue making them and donating them to the hospice center that took care of his mother.

Using his own key to the front door of the ranch-style house, he walked in calling out, "Hey, I'm here."

He followed the sound of their voices to the kitchen.

"You're late," Marc said when Jonathan walked into the kitchen.

"I was tied up."

"I heard," his brother replied.

"I know you're not going to come in here and not speak," a woman yelled out.

Seeing one of his aunts, he went over to where she sat.

"Hey, Auntie Anna," he said, kissing her cheek.

She pushed him away, saying, "Don't be trying to get all sweet with me . . . trying to give me some sugah so we won't work your tongue out today."

"Get over here, boy, and give me some if Anna doesn't want it."

"How are you, Auntie?" Jonathan asked, going over to his Aunt Bertha.

"Auntie's fine. Just a little pain in this here knee, but I don't let it keep me down. Gotta keep moving."

"I hear ya," Jonathan said, smiling brightly.

Jonathan went over to his Aunt Rachel and gave her a kiss.

Rachel Damon was a tall, thin, chestnut-brown-skinned woman with short salt-and-pepper hair. She and her husband, Isaiah, raised him and Marc after the deaths of their mother and father. He'd always have a special place in his heart for them.

"I didn't think you were going to come; you haven't come to visit in a while." Rachel looked up at him.

Before Jonathan could respond, his Aunt Anna piped up.

"Yeah, must be sniffing around some woman."

Jonathan quickly denied the suggestion. "Why would you say that, Auntie?"

"You should bring her around," Annie said.

"Annie, he must be ashamed of us, then," Bertha chimed in.

"Sister, he's not. He's just been busy," Rachel said.

Anna peered over the top of her cat-eye glasses. "When are you going to get married?"

Rachel continued working with the pink square fabric on her side.

"Anna, don't start. He's got plenty of time to marry."

Anna sighed. She looked over in Jonathan's direction. "I'm sorry, sweetie, I didn't mean to give you a hard time."

"It's all right, Auntie," Jonathan said, wishing he could tell them that he was already married.

Anna paused before continuing. "I must say, though, that I'll be glad when you do."

Bertha teared up. "I know your momma would be proud of both you boys. Marc's wife is a lovely girl."

"Okay, Aunt Rachel, you wanted me to come over to help you."

Rachel got up and pressed the button to change the CD on the player that was mounted under one of the kitchen cabinets. The distinct sound of Pastor Shirley Caesar wafted through the room.

They all fell into a nice rhythm.

"Sing, Shirley!" Bertha exclaimed, pulling the thread out of the fabric and rocking back and forth to the beat of the music.

"How did you ladies learn how to quilt?" Jonathan asked.

"We learned when we were little girls," the aunts replied in unison.

"We used to make some of the prettiest quilts. Your momma used to help us, too, God rest her soul," Anna added.

Jonathan looked at the boxes on the floor filled with quilts. "How many of these do you guys have to make, Aunt Rachel?" he asked.

"We are making three for this month. Then we'll start on new ones for the next month," Bertha responded.

"There are so many people who have this dreaded disease; we want to be a blessing to as many as we can." Rachel said, smoothing out the patch she worked on.

"You have to know what you're doing, though, boy," Anna pointed out.

"How long have you been here?" Jonathan asked Marc.

"Twenty minutes before you arrived."

"I can't believe how fast they are," Jonathan said as he bent down and picked up one of the fancy covers from the box on the floor.

Jonathan figured out that his aunt really didn't want anything; she only wanted to see him. "Well, where is Uncle Isaiah?" Jonathan asked.

"You didn't see him outside in the garage?" Rachel asked, sounding concerned.

"No, his car was there, but I didn't see him," Jonathan said, he and Marc both seeing the sudden panic in their aunt's eyes. Marc left immediately, while Jonathan stopped to hug his aunt, saying, "Don't worry, we'll check things out."

Jonathan ran out the side door and around to the back and found Marc trying to open the garage door. "Why didn't you get the remote control?"

"Why didn't you?" Jonathan asked, running back into the house through the side door into the house and pressing the button from the inside.

When he got back outside, he heard his brother calling him and ran in the direction of his voice to the side of the garage.

Their uncle was lying on the ground, and Marc was supporting his upper body.

"Is he hurt? What happened?"

With a dismissive wave of his hand Isaiah said, "Oh, hell, I'm all right. I just missed a step on the ladder when I was coming down."

"I thought Aunt Rachel told you to stay off ladders," Jonathan said as he and Marc helped to test his reflexes.

"I was trying fix that gutter. It was trying to come away from the house."

"Aunt Rachel has asked us to help you with some things around here, but she didn't go into any detail," Jonathan said.

"Maybe she wanted us to fix the gutter and not you," Marc speculated.

"Help me into the garage; I need to rest a minute before we go back inside," Isaiah said, in effect admitting that he was at least winded.

When they reached the front of the garage, Jonathan got a folding lawn chair for his uncle.

"Rachel wanted both you boys close to her."

Jonathan and Marc looked puzzled. "What do you mean?"

Pulling himself forward, Isaiah reached over and rubbed his hand over Jonathan's close-cropped hair. "She feels that you don't come over to see us as much as you used to. Since sonny boy over here got married, you don't come over for dinner."

Then it hit Jonathan. She was jealous.

"Don't tell me Auntie is jealous," he said, surprised.

Moving his head vigorously, Isaiah said, "No, she's not jealous. It's just sometimes she gets a little emotional when it comes to you two. We never had kids of our own, and after your mother and then my brother died, both of you belonged to us. We got the children we always wanted, but we both lost our siblings. It was a bittersweet experience."

The brothers fell silent for several moments, and then Jonathan spoke.

"Let's go inside before she comes out here looking for us. She was already concerned because I told her I hadn't seen you out here when I drove up."

When they got inside, Rachel ran over to Isaiah, asking, "Where were you?"

Isaiah kissed Rachel on the lips in response.

"Isaiah Damon, you were out there on that ladder again, weren't you?"

Isaiah only smiled.

Rachel rolled her eyes and went back to piecing together the fabric squares without another word. But Marc and Jonathan were not off the hook.

"Okay, boys, I want you to take these boxes out to Bertha's car," she said.

Jonathan picked up one of the boxes and headed for the door. As he walked down the sidewalk to the car, he thought about the tacit exchange between his aunt and uncle and admired the way his uncle communicated with his wife without words. Clearly, there was a real love between them. He wondered if he and Ivy could ever have that kind of love and understanding.

CHAPTER 18

It only took Ivy ten minutes to arrive at Violet's house. She turned off the ignition, but didn't move. She sat staring out of the driver's side window for a few moments.

She reached over and lifted her purse from the floor. After pulling her key from the ignition, she got out of the car and walked up to the front door.

Ringing the bell, she waited for Violet to answer.

"That was quick," Violet said, opening the door.

Violet and Ivy were both the same height. They looked more alike than their other two sisters, with their coffee-colored skin and statuesque frames. The only difference was in their hairstyles: Ivy wore hers pulled back in a chignon most of the time, and Violet sported a short haircut.

"We need to talk," Ivy said as she walked past Violet and into the house.

"I'm making soup, so come on in the kitchen and we can talk there."

Violet had just moved into her roomy two-bedroom brick house a year ago. The home had an open floor plan with cathedral ceilings with big windows for a larger appearance.

"Aren't you going to take off your coat? Or is this so serious that you think I'm going to kick you out after I hear it?" Violet said, walking into the kitchen behind her.

"I'm good," Ivy said as she pulled her purse from her shoulder and sat it on the floor beside her.

Ivy admired the way Violet had decorated the kitchen. The cranberry-colored walls went perfectly with the custom whitewashed oak wood cabinets, granite countertops, stainless steel appliances and tiled center island and floor.

The large wooden cutting board had a giant knife and lots of celery, carrots and onions cut into little pieces laying on it.

Ivy sat on the stool at the island and picked up a carrot. Violet sat on the other side across from her.

"All right, Vee, spit it out. What's going on with you that's so serious that you had to rush over to talk?"

Ivy leaned forward and said, "I want to tell you something, but you have to promise me that you won't tell another living soul."

Violet split open a piece of celery and glanced up at her sister. "You know I won't say anything, Vee. What do you think I'm going to do, stand out in the middle of the street and tell it to the neighborhood?" Violet chuckled.

Ivy frowned. "Violet, I'm not joking. This is very serious. We're talking about my life here."

Violet laid the knife down on the cutting board, reached across the island and squeezed her sister's hand gently. "Okay, Vee. I promise I won't tell anyone."

"Not even Rose, and especially not big-mouth Lili."

Violet nodded. "I won't tell Lili, either." She went back to chopping up the vegetables. "Man, Vee, you act like you're going to tell me that you have hit the lottery or that you and Jonathan are getting married. You've only gone on a couple of dates," she joked, chopping up an onion now.

"We're already married," Ivy blurted out.

Violet almost sliced her finger instead of the celery.

"You are lying to me," she said in disbelief.

Ivy merely shook her head from side to side.

Dropping the utensil, Violet rushed around to the other side of the island and grabbed Ivy.

"Tell me you're playing. You're kidding, right? Vee, what is the matter with you?" She looked Ivy in the eye.

"Remember, you can't tell anyone," Ivy reminded her. She realized that her sister was still in shock by the way she stared at her with her mouth hung open.

Ivy turned away in embarrassment. "Don't look at me like that. It was a mistake."

"Mistake? Vee, you're a rational thinker. You help people get married for a living. You know how this goes. You can't marry someone by mistake, especially when you have to say I do, I will, or something of the sort."

"You can if you're drunk."

Violet rolled her eyes. "You were *what*? What has gotten into you?" Her voice raised an octave.

"I'm going to get an annulment," Ivy threw in.

Violet waved her hands. "Wait, wait. I know I've got to be missing something, or there is something you aren't

telling me. I think you need to start from the beginning."
She sat on the stool next to her sister.

Ivy heard the pot boiling on the stove. "Don't you think you should see about your pot?"

Violet ran over to the stove, quickly turning the heat down under the huge stainless steel container. Taking the lid off, she reached for the cutting board, racking all the cut up vegetables into the pot before returning the lid.

She rushed back over to Ivy. "Okay, spill it, sister. I want to understand exactly what happened." Violet shook her head before saying, "I can't believe that you married Jonathan."

"At first I couldn't believe it, either, but now I could see why I would."

As she watched the confusion wash over her sister's face, she realized she needed to fully explain.

"Let me tell you." Ivy told Violet the whole story, from her chance meeting Jonathan at the airport to her having a few too many drinks, to her waking up married.

Once she'd brought her up to speed, Violet, still in amazement, spoke to her.

"How long do you have before it's too late to get an annulment?"

"One year."

"But now you're saying that you're having second thoughts about the marriage. Is it because you've been sleeping with him?"

Ivy's mouth flew open and she shook her head vigorously. She was torn between conflicting emotions.

"It's not that at all. We've been spending a lot of time together and I like who I am when I'm with him. He's so easy to be with, and I laugh. He is the sweetest guy."

"I understand that. I think he's sweet, too, but enough to marry him?"

Ivy's eyes filled with tears. "I love him, Violet."

Violet's eyes widened. "You do? Well then, that's another story. How does Jonathan feel about being married to you?"

"He said he didn't think us getting married was a bad idea."

Violet nodded. "Oh. You need to see where the relationship takes you. We all knew he was interested in you, so I think you should give it an honest chance."

Ivy nodded. "I have until December."

She gave her sister a warning stare. "Remember Violet, you can't tell anyone."

Violet crossed her heart and said, "I promise I won't breathe a word."

Ivy got up. "I needed to get that off my chest."

"Why don't you stay until the soup gets ready? I can show you some of the dress sketches I've been working on."

"Sure."

Violet reached over and hugged Ivy. "You'll make the right decision. Don't worry, things are going to work out."

Several hours later, Ivy went home and prepared to take a hot bubble bath. She sat on the side of the tub, trailing her finger through the thick bubbles that formed from the champagne-and-strawberry-scented bubble bath she had poured under the running water.

She had taken off her clothes and had put on her silk robe over her pink lacy bra and panties. As she waited for the tub to fill, her mind drifted to Jonathan and the conversation she'd had with Violet.

Would she make the right decision about him? Will he let her down like Randall did? She didn't know, but what she did know was that she loved him and it felt good.

Turning off the water she untied her robe, letting it slip to the floor before removing her panties and bra.

She stepped into the hot water and sank down until the bubbles reached her collarbone. Lying back against her clam-shaped terry-cloth bath pillow, she relaxed.

CHAPTER 19

Jonathan waited until it was closer to ten o'clock before he went over to Hearts and Flowers. He admitted to himself that he couldn't wait to meet Randall Holloway. He wanted to look the man who broke Ivy's heart in the face. He wondered what kind of man would ask a woman whom he supposedly loved to get rid of their child . . . his seed. He had to be a cold-hearted man.

He recognized the silver SUV parked in the lot as he pulled into the empty space across from it. Lauren Kabins sat on the passenger side. The man driving the automobile had to be Randall.

Jonathan stared at Randall, watching him and Lauren in conversation. He waited until they got out of their vehicle before exiting his. As soon as she climbed out, Lauren recognized him.

"Jonathan," she called out.

Jonathan turned around and walked toward her. Holding out his hand to her, he said, "Lauren, how have you been?" Jonathan focused on Lauren, but could see Randall walking up next to her.

"I'm great. I came over for the cake tasting today." Lauren smiled and asked, "What are you doing over here?"

This time instead of Jonathan looking at Lauren, he turned and glared at Randall before answering, "I came to help out a friend."

Lauren turned to her right. "Jonathan, I'd like you to meet my fiancé, Randall Holloway."

Randall extended his hand to Jonathan. "Nice to meet you."

Jonathan stared at his hand for a moment and then extended his. "Yeah, nice to meet you, too," he said coolly.

Randall gave Jonathan a puzzled stare before taking Lauren by the arm and walking away.

Ivy sat at her desk waiting for Lauren and Randall to show up for their ten o'clock appointment. She reflected on the thoughtful gesture Jonathan made that morning, when he called to remind her that he would be there. Even though she didn't worry about Randall causing a commotion, she appreciated Jonathan's support.

The intercom buzzed. "Yes, Gwen."

"Lauren Kabins and her fiancé are here."

"I'll be right down."

Ivy walked swiftly out of her office and down the hall to the reception area.

Once she got closer, she saw Gwen taking their coats and Jonathan standing off to the side, his eyes on Randall. He had made it just as he promised. She went to him, and before she could say anything he kissed her. "Hey, baby."

Ivy grabbed his hand and whispered, "Thank you."

She started walking away, and he finally released her hand.

"Good morning, you two." Ivy glanced at Randall and saw the unreadable look that marred his face. She decided to ignore it. She stopped in front of Lauren first. "Good morning. How are you?"

Lauren and Ivy hugged each other.

Stepping out of her embrace, Ivy asked, "Are you ready to eat some cake?"

"Violet called me this morning to tell me that my dress has been shipped. I guess I'll have it in a couple of days."

"Everything is coming right along. I don't see anything that would stop us from getting you married on time."

The two women walked down the hall together, leaving Randall behind them, Jonathan trailing after him.

Walking into the foyer of Lili's office suite, there was a comfortable couch and a mahogany cocktail table laden with books and magazines about cakes. They walked through another doorway into the cake display room.

Lauren pointed at a towering confection of chocolate that was on display. "Wow, that is simply gorgeous," she said to Randall, who didn't express his opinion. He kept looking behind him and seeing Jonathan there.

"These are what we call dummy cakes. We decorate them and put them on display for brides to view," Ivy said as they waited for Lili, who was on the telephone.

As she entered the room, Lili greeted everyone. "Good morning."

Everybody responded to Lili's greeting except Randall. Ivy watched him glance at his watch for the third time since they'd been in the room.

"Randall, do you have another appointment?"

Randall glared at her. "No, why?"

"Oh, I'm sorry. You keep looking at the time."

Lili stepped up. "Well, we aren't going to keep you. If you follow me this way, I have the cakes already set up for you to taste. We can finalize the cake order and you can be on your way."

Everyone went into an area that had been set up with all the amenities of a commercial kitchen: an oven, prep tables, supply racks and a marble-top table that seated six.

Lili set the table with four small dessert plates, forks, and napkins. In the middle of the table sat two platters, each having four different slices of cake.

"Have a seat and we can get started," she offered.

Lauren and Randall sat down next to Lili, Ivy sat on the other side and Jonathan hung in the shadows.

"Couples today are experimenting with different flavors and shapes so that they will have a unique cake to present to their guests at the wedding reception." She looked at Lauren. "I think you've chosen a wonderful design. Today we are going to choose the flavor and fillings for those cakes. The flavor is an integral part as it gives the taste and color to the cake. We offer twenty-seven different flavors, but based on the information you gave to Ivy, I chose four."

She pointed. "This is the white butter cake made with fresh sweet butter. You can combine this cake with the vanilla, grand marnier, fresh citrus, or white or dark chocolate flavors. I chose the white chocolate for today."

Lauren picked up her fork and broke off a piece. "Hmm, this is good." She broke off another piece and put it in front of Randall. He bent and opened his mouth to taste.

"Do you like it?" Lauren asked.

Randall hunched his shoulders. "It's okay. You pick. I don't have to taste any more."

Ivy could see by the expression on Lauren's face that Randall had hurt her feelings.

Ivy reached across the table and grabbed Lauren's hand. "With so many choices, it can be a bit overwhelming, but concentrate on what you like," she said, trying to comfort the young woman.

Lili tried as well. She picked up the platter again and said, "Try this one. It's one of my favorites."

Lauren cut a small piece of the rich-looking chocolate cake.

"Good?" Lili asked.

Lauren closed her eyes, savoring the flavor. "I love this one. What do you call it?"

"This is made with extra dark cocoa and a hint of spice. You can combine this with flavored Swiss meringue butter cream filled with vanilla, chocolate, and mocha. This one is espresso mocha."

Ivy suspected something was going on with Randall. When he should have been paying attention to Lauren, he was watching Jonathan.

And from the time she'd come to greet them at the reception desk, Jonathan's eyes had been on Randall.

Ivy wondered if something happened between them. But she was sure Randall and Jonathan didn't know each other. Jonathan only knew what she'd told him about Randall.

Randall pulled out his cell phone. He got up from the table and bent down to give Lauren a kiss on the lips. "Babe, I need to take this phone call, and I have a couple of questions for Ivy."

Ivy blinked. She had no idea what he was talking about. She watched him walk toward the door.

"Ivy, can I talk to you for a minute?"

When Ivy got up and walked over to him, Jonathan, who had been standing near the door, turned and followed her.

Randall stopped when they entered the hallway. He looked Jonathan in the eye. "I'd like to speak to Ms. Hart alone, if you don't mind."

Jonathan took a step forward, but Ivy pulled the tail of his suit jacket.

"If you have a question about cake costs, Randall, you should have asked Lili."

"Let's just go to the office and I can explain."

Ivy walked to her office with Randall, leaving Jonathan in the hall.

As soon as they entered the office, Randall started raising his voice. "Who is this Jonathan guy?"

Ivy sat in the chair behind her desk. "I don't understand the question."

"Jonathan, the cat that kissed you and who has been sticking around all morning."

"A friend."

"How long have you known him?"

"Why, Randall?"

"How does he know Lauren, and why is he following us like he's security?"

"Your wedding is taking place at his banquet hall. And I don't think he's following you, he's here for me."

"Yeah, right," Randall snapped.

"If you had questions about Jonathan, then you should have asked him. We were all in the same room." Leaning forward, Ivy asked, "Why the inquisition?"

Randall's eyes narrowed. He leaned over her desk as close as he could without leaving his chair. "You told him about what happened between us, didn't you?"

Randall jumped up from his seat. Fire danced in his eyes as he quickly ran around to the other side of the desk. Leaning closer to Ivy, he said through gritted teeth. "I knew that's why that SOB looked at me funny."

Ivy pushed her chair back, making him move out of the way. "What I tell my friends is none of your business."

He slammed his fist against her desk. "It is if it's going to ruin my marriage. You had no right. I know you told him, Ivy. Can I trust him? I don't want him whispering lies to Lauren."

"What do you mean, lies? I didn't tell him any lies."

Randall blew out an aggravated breath, and then pointed to Ivy. "You're trying to get back at me. Payback is a mutha." Randall eyed her intensely. "I'm not going to let you ruin my life."

"Back up, bruh." Jonathan rushed over, pulling Randall away from Ivy's desk.

Randall pushed him back and was straightening out his suit when Lauren ran in.

"What are you doing, Randall?" she cried out.

Randall rushed over to her. "Nothing, baby, Ms. Hart and I were having a conversation."

"If it was nothing, then why were you pushing Jonathan?"

Randall was silent.

"I hope you're not going to act this way every time a man speaks to me or pays me a compliment. I don't think I could handle a jealous husband."

Randall glared at Jonathan. "I'm not jealous of this man."

Ivy pulled Jonathan back when he stepped forward.

"It's not worth it," she whispered.

Lauren walked over and stood next to Ivy's desk. "Ivy, can you tell me what's going on?"

Ivy reached out and touched Lauren's shoulder. "I'm sorry, sweetheart, but you need to talk to Randall about that."

Lauren turned to him. "Randall?"

Randall rushed over to her and said, "Baby, let me explain."

Lauren moved to the side out of his way. "Explain," she said calmly at first, then she screamed, "Explain."

Ivy grabbed Jonathan's hand and they started to walk from the room. "We're going to give you two some time alone."

Lauren held up her hand. "No, I don't think so. I think you're involved in this somehow. What really happened between you and Randall?"

"I don't know what you're talking about."

"You know exactly what I mean," Lauren shouted, glancing between Ivy and Randall.

Jonathan walked over to Lauren. "I understand that you're upset, because you don't know what's going on. But, Lauren, I agree with Ivy. This is between you and Randall." He gave Randall an unpleasant gaze. "If anyone should tell you anything, it should be him."

Jonathan reached for Ivy's hand and started walking away, but stopped in front of Randall. "Handle your business, man." Then he said to Lauren, "We'll let you two have your privacy."

Bringing Ivy's hand to his lips, he kissed it and they walked out of the office, leaving the couple alone.

Jonathan and Ivy walked upstairs to the conference room. Once inside, Jonathan removed a chair from under the table and sat down first and then pulled Ivy down onto his lap.

"Are you okay?" Jonathan asked her, rubbing her shoulders.

Ivy pressed her forehead against his. "I'm fine. Thank you for being here today."

Jonathan kissed her softly on the lips. "If he'd gotten any closer, I would have popped him upside his head."

Ivy played with the knot in his tie. "I'm glad it didn't come to that. I just think Randall is scared for whatever reason."

"What do you think is going to happen between those two?"

Ivy shook her head. "I don't know, but I'm not going to worry about it. Let Randall slay his own giant."

CHAPTER 20

Ivy checked her watch and stood. She and Jonathan had been sitting in the conference room for the last fifteen minutes. He needed to leave, and she needed to see what was happening with Lauren and Randall.

"Let's go and see what happened," she said to Jonathan.

As they walked down the stairs, they saw Gwen coming toward them.

"Ivy, I was looking for you."

"I was in the conference room," she said, continuing to walk toward her office.

"Lauren Kabins told me to tell you that she'll call you tomorrow."

"Did she and her fiancé leave?" Ivy wanted to know.

"Yes, they both left about five minutes ago."

Ivy looked at Jonathan and then back at Gwen. "Thanks a lot, Gwen."

As soon as Gwen was out of earshot, Jonathan said to Ivy, "I wonder what happened?"

"I guess we'll find out tomorrow." Ivy shook her head and continued to her office. "We'd better make sure the office isn't a wreck."

There was a possibility that Lauren had thrown something or pushed something over to release her frustration, anger and disappointment. Ivy canvassed the room, but everything was in its place.

"Things are fine here," Jonathan said, inspecting the place himself.

"True. Looks that way, doesn't it?" Ivy said, picking up the folder from the desk. "Well, looks can be deceiving. We've just got to wait and see."

An uneasy feeling swept over Ivy as she remembered the look of disappointment on Lauren's face when she'd left the office. The excited and vibrant young woman she'd met a couple of weeks ago had been replaced with a woman filled with uncertainty.

Jonathan bent to give Ivy a kiss. "I hate that things turned out this way."

"If Randall hadn't harped on the situation, Lauren would have never found out."

"But, baby, like you said, we don't know what Randall said to her."

"You're right, but I've got this weird feeling we're going find out soon."

After Jonathan left, Ivy placed an order for wedding invitations and favors for two brides who were getting married in May and June. She'd picked up the phone several times to call Lauren, but she only got as far as dialing the first three numbers before hanging up. She would wait until Lauren contacted her.

"Girl, this has been a day."

Lili came strolling into the office, throwing her body into the chair in front of Ivy's desk.

"Yes, it has been interesting," Ivy said as she turned to type a note in the brides file.

"Vee, what did Randall want?"

"Not a thing." Ivy didn't lie, but she didn't need to go into details about her conversation with Randall, especially not with Lili.

"Let me tell you, when you left the room, Lauren had this look on her face like 'why does he have to talk to Ivy in private'." She waved her hand. "I was thinking to myself, 'Uh, oh, it's about to jump off in here.' "

Ivy shook her head. "You're exaggerating, Lili."

Lili sat up straight in the chair, pushing herself to the edge. "No, I'm not. She kept looking back at the door. I had to keep trying to get her to focus on what we were doing. So finally when she'd made her choices, she said 'I'm going to go and see what's taking them so long.'"

Ivy stared at her sister, wondering if Lili knew how much she talked and how fast she did it.

Getting up from her desk, she went to the bookcase and removed a reference manual and brought it back.

"All I can say is once she entered this office, Jonathan and I were certain they needed to talk to each other alone."

Lili grabbed the arms of the chair and brought it closer to her sister's wide desk. "Oh, yeah, I was meaning to ask you about Jonathan. Why was he here?"

What was she going to do with her sister? As soon as she answered one question, thinking it would be the end, Lili came back with another.

"You should have been a news reporter instead of a baker."

Lili tucked one leg underneath the other. "I'm just trying to get the facts."

Ivy glanced at her watch. "Don't you have other appointments today?"

Lili checked hers as well before standing to her feet. "I sure do. I have two this afternoon. Rosie and I are going out for lunch. Do you want to come with us?"

A wide smile suddenly appeared on Ivy's face. She had gotten used to Lili's tricks. If she wanted to play twenty questions, she'd agree to lunch, but she'd already played that game with her sister.

"Thanks, sweetie, but I've got to catch up."

Lili strolled toward the office door before turning back to Ivy. "Maybe next time. And you still didn't answer my question as to why Jonathan was here, but that's okay. I'll check you later."

Ivy chuckled and went back to work, but was immediately interrupted again by the ringing of the telephone.

"Vee, have you got a minute?"

"Sure, Rosie."

"I'm coming down there. I don't want to say this over the phone."

"I thought you were going to lunch with Lili."

"I am, but I need to talk to you first."

Ivy hung up and waited for Rose.

"Vee, did you know that Gwen was engaged?"

Ivy's eyes narrowed. "No. When did this happen?"

"I overheard her talking to her mother on the phone. She was saying something about not having the money to spend on a big wedding."

"Hmm," Ivy said, trying to figure out what the words could mean.

Leaning forward, she clasped her hands together. "You know what, Rosie, we shouldn't say anything to her because she may not want us to know."

Rose shook her head. "I understand that, but maybe we can help her. She works here. We're supposed be one of the best in the business. Why not help her?"

"We'll help her. Let me just think of a way we can do it without looking nosey."

Rose stood to her feet. "I'd better get going or Lili will be looking for me."

Rose left her office, and Ivy hoped she wouldn't have any more interruptions. She wanted to get a bite to eat herself because her afternoon would be just as busy.

Ivy called in her lunch order, went and picked it up and ate while she finished her column for the next week and reviewed the seating chart for Lauren's wedding. She'd gotten a steady flow of responses, and put individuals together based on the list Lauren had given her.

After she e-mailed her column to the editor, Ivy received a call from Sally Carter wanting to know if Ivy would come into the studio in the morning to shoot a promo for the reality show. They set the appointment for nine o'clock.

Ivy sat and reflected on her life. So much had happened since the start of the new year. She couldn't have imagined giving wedding planning advice to couples on a television program, writing a newspaper column and getting married.

She thought the last one would destroy her, but it turned out to be one of her greatest blessings. She couldn't have imagined a better friend than Jonathan. When she flew home from Las Vegas, Jonathan was a problem that she had to get rid of before anyone else found out, but now she wanted to shout it from the rooftops that she was Mrs. Jonathan Damon.

Because of her experience with Randall, fear of rejection and disappointment had plagued her each and every time any other man tried to get close to her. She'd then have to find a way to get out of the relationship. She liked her life the way it was, and letting a man get to know her intimately meant taking a chance with her heart. Ivy hadn't risked it in a very, very long time.

The way Jonathan came into her life wasn't ideal, but she felt good about her decision to let Jonathan in. Their special relationship had been like non-other she'd had in her life.

Ivy picked up her phone and dialed Jonathan's number. "Hey, babe."

"I'm inviting you over tonight."

"You are?"

"I just want to celebrate us. Nothing fancy, but something that will make us appreciate each other."

"Hmmm," he said. "This sounds like a seduction to me. I like the way you said 'appreciate each other'. Ivy, what are you going to do to me?"

"Just come over at about seven," Ivy said, ignoring his last question.

"I'll be there."

"What kind of pizza do you like?" she asked.

"Beef sausage and pepperoni," Jonathan said, adding, "Why don't I bring the pizza?"

"Sure, but I like thin crust," Ivy said.

"I'll see you tonight at about seven o'clock," he said to Ivy.

"I'm looking forward to it."

As soon as she ended the call, Ivy replayed the sexy way Jonathan's voice sounded. Desire washed through her, and she couldn't wait to see him.

Music and candlelight filled the house when Jonathan arrived. Suspicion rose within him when Ivy came to the door and disappeared.

He put the pizza on the kitchen countertop and went looking for her.

"Where are you?" he asked, walking into the great room and down the hall.

"I'm back here," he heard her yell.

Jonathan strolled down the long hall to her bedroom.

"You disappeared . . ." His words fell off as soon as he walked into the room and saw her rubbing her naked body with a scented lotion.

He eyed her perky round breasts and her naked thighs resting against the bed linen, and was tempted to forget the pizza. He went over and sat beside her.

Ivy couldn't help laughing; she knew what he was thinking the moment she looked into his eyes.

"Let me finish this so we can eat."

Ignoring her, Jonathan pulled the bobby pins from her hair, which she'd pinned up to avoid getting it wet in the shower.

"Jonathan," she said softly.

"I think we should finish this first," he said, "and then we can eat."

He picked up the tube of vanilla scented lotion and squeezed a dollop into his hand. He rubbed his hands together and then massaged the creamy mixture into her shoulders.

Ivy couldn't help herself; she leaned back on her elbows and allowed herself to revel in his sensuous strokes. She almost forgot she was completely naked.

Jonathan got up and kneeled in front of her, taking the lotion with him. Starting with her feet, he began to massage her. He then went to her legs and massaged them before parting her thighs and rubbing them with the lotion.

After hearing her moans, Jonathan's need to take off his blue jeans became urgent, but he decided to wait; this was her moment.

With her legs spread, Jonathan gently caressed the curls concealing her essence. Looking up at her, he knew exactly what she needed.

"Lie back," he whispered, his voice ragged.

Closing her eyes, Ivy did exactly what he asked. She knew what happened next was going to be good.

Jonathan lifted Ivy's round bottom and grasped her thighs, drawing her body toward him. He planted kisses on the inside of her thighs, slowly moving downward and getting closer and closer to her most sensitive spot.

Caught by surprise, her eyes flew open and she began to squirm. She had not anticipated what he was about to do.

Feeling her discomfort, Jonathan paused, saying, "Relax, baby, and let me love you."

And Ivy did just that; she let Jonathan love her. They made love to each other, and neither thought about the time or the pizza, now probably stone cold.

Resting in Jonathan's embrace, her hand on his chest, Ivy watched him, thinking he was asleep.

"What is it?" he asked, opening his eyes slightly.

"I thought you were asleep," she replied, kissing him on the side of the mouth.

"Look, woman, don't start. I'll flip you over and be inside you before you take your next breath."

Ivy smiled. She knew he meant every word. "I wanted to call Lauren a couple of times today, but I just couldn't."

Jonathan turned to face her. "I thought about her today myself. I couldn't help but wonder what he said to her. She seemed like a sweet girl."

"Yes, a woman in love. I keep telling myself that I shouldn't be concerned, but I just can't help it."

Jonathan kissed her nose. "In our line of work, it's inevitable because we actually share in some of the most memorable moments in people's lives."

Ivy hugged him. "That is true, but before I just made sure that the magic was there. I didn't get all emotional about it."

"Or so you thought," Jonathan said, interrupting her.

"Maybe I feel so differently because it was somebody from my own past."

Jonathan lifted a stray curl off her face. "That's probably part of it, but you are passionate about every wedding you put together. Look at how sad it made you feel when the first couple of your show broke off their engagement."

He pulled her close and caressed her naked bottom. "As I said, you are a passionate woman. I always knew that, but now I've experienced it."

Ivy kissed him and laid her head against his shoulder. After a while, she tried to roll to the other side of the bed.

"Where do you think you're going?" he asked, pulling her back.

"Aren't you hungry?"

"For you, always."

Ivy punched him playfully. "I meant for food." She finally managed to get up and out of the bed, going over to a chair to get her silk robe.

"I'm going to warm up the pizza. You want some?"

Jonathan rested his hand behind his head. "I guess I could eat something. I am going to need my strength for later."

Ivy smiled and shook her head. "You are a mess."

Jonathan beamed. "I'm glad you know it."

Ivy was about to cross the threshold when Jonathan said something unexpected.

"No more sleeping in separate houses. I want to go to bed with you and see your face when I wake up in the morning."

Ivy didn't know what to say, wondering why he was telling her that now. She was already confused about the whole situation and wasn't ready to make a decision, so she just smiled and left the room.

CHAPTER 21

After Ivy completed the promo for the show, she went to Sally's office to talk about some questions she'd had concerning the next segment they were scheduled to shoot over the next couple of days.

Ivy thought some of the changes Sally made went against the wishes of the bride and groom. As she listened to the woman's reasoning, Ivy found out that some reality shows had little to do with reality. She would make the best of it.

As she left the studio, she dug down in her purse to find her car keys and saw the screen of her cell phone was illuminated; she'd missed several calls.

Reviewing the call history, she discovered that they were all from her office. She walked swiftly to her car and called once she was inside.

"Ivy," Gwen said, answering the phone quickly without reciting their normal greeting.

Ivy's heartbeat accelerated after hearing the panic in the receptionist's voice. "Did something happen?"

"Yes, you need to call Lauren Kabins right away."

What has this fool done to this girl now, Ivy thought to herself. She hoped Randall hadn't told Lauren a ridiculous lie to save his own behind.

The next thing that caught her attention was the way in which Gwen had been conducting herself. She didn't like it when simple things were blown out of proportion. Lauren had told her she would call, so she didn't see why the panic. "Gwen, is that the only reason you've called me five times this morning?" There was a pregnant pause before Ivy spoke up. "Girl, you sounded like a pipe had busted and the place was flooded or Lili blew up the kitchen or something. Don't scare me like that again."

Both women were silent and then they both laughed. "Ivy, I'm sorry, Lauren sounded distraught and every time she'd call, I told her you were out of the office. We'd hang up, but she'd call right back. So I just called you every time she called us."

Ivy pushed her key in the ignition and turned it. "Well, I'm going to call her now. I'm on my way back to the office."

"Okay," Gwen said.

"Gwen."

"Yes?"

"Calm down, girl. We've been doing this kind of work a long time now. I thought you would have been used to bridal pandemonium."

"You're right, I'm sorry. I'll see you when you get here."

Ivy completed the call and dialed Lauren's phone number. Plugging her headset in, she pulled out of the parking lot and drove back to Hearts and Flowers as she waited for Lauren to answer. She didn't answer, so Ivy left a voicemail message.

It took Ivy forty-five minutes to get back to her office from Chicago. She suddenly felt optimistic when she pulled into her parking space and spotted Lauren's car in the lot.

Almost immediately Gwen spoke as soon as Ivy walked in the door. "Lauren came in as soon as we hung up."

"Where is she?" Ivy asked.

Gwen pointed straight ahead in the direction of the waiting area.

Ivy shook her head and kept a smile on her face. "Thanks, Gwen, I'll handle it from here." When she walked away from the desk, she thought Gwen's ultra-hyper activity was weird because she was normally a charming and pleasant young lady.

Ivy took several deep breaths as she walked the short distance to the waiting room. Once she came upon the threshold of the door, her heart dropped. Lauren was crying. Not a loud, wailing cry, but the tears were running down her cheeks as she sat in the armchair over in the corner.

Compassion and disappointment came over Ivy when she saw her this way.

"Lauren," Ivy said softly.

Lauren stood and inhaled deeply in an effort to control her emotions. Ivy went to her, wrapping her arms around her shoulders, and said, "Why don't we talk in my office?"

Lauren followed Ivy, continuing to dab her face with the handkerchief and didn't say a word.

Both women sat in the chairs in front of Ivy's desk.

"Lauren," Ivy reached over and placed her hand on Lauren's knee.

Lauren looked up.

"Did you come for your dress fitting?" Ivy wanted to sound optimistic. Ivy had her own opinion as to why, but she figured she shouldn't jump to conclusions. There could have been several reasons that Lauren cried.

Ivy stood to her feet, picked up Lauren's hand and encouraged her to stand as well.

Pulling the petite young woman into her arms, she hugged her for several minutes. Ivy felt the jerking in Lauren's chest and the whimpers that escaped her mouth.

There was a little guilt attached to Ivy's feelings, and she hoped she didn't contribute to Lauren's pain.

She led her over to the sitting area and they sat down next to each other on the sofa.

"Why did you come to see me today?" Ivy asked, her voice soft, filled with concern.

"I'm canceling my wedding," Lauren finally said.

Before Ivy responded, she thought about her words carefully. She didn't want to say the wrong thing, nor did she want to pry. She would accept whatever Lauren told her. After all, it was her life and her decision. Allowing someone else to influence your decision about your life was unacceptable, and Ivy knew that feeling very well.

"Have you discussed this with Randall?"

"Yes, I told him that he could go overseas by himself. I didn't want to live in Japan anyway. Since I'm an only child, I didn't want to be that far away from my mother."

Both women sat quietly until Lauren broke the silence. "I think he's keeping things from me. He kept dancing around the subject of your relationship with him."

Ivy swallowed hard. Because she didn't know what Randall shared with Lauren, she'd have to be careful how she responded to the statement.

"My relationship with him?"

"Yes. I could hear him yelling as I got closer to your office, and I stopped outside the door. I wanted to hear what he had to say for myself, before I came in."

Ivy nodded and said, "I see." There wasn't more to be said.

"I know you two had a relationship in the past, but that's not the reason I'm canceling the wedding. It's the way he handled the entire situation."

Ivy saw the tears appear in Lauren's eyes as she explained.

"The anger and rage that he showed yesterday scared me. I started to wonder if this was the same man I fell in love with almost a year ago. If Jonathan hadn't come in when he did, what would have happened? Would he have hit you?"

"Sweetie, I can't answer that."

"I couldn't answer it, either. But I gave him the benefit of the doubt."

"Before you brought him here a couple of weeks ago, I hadn't seen or heard from Randall in over ten years."

"Ten years?"

"Yes. Once we broke up I stayed away, and once I graduated I moved back here."

With tears spilling down her cheeks, Lauren continued, "It's what happened after you and Jonathan left that drove the nail in his coffin, so to speak."

"What did he say?"

"It's what he didn't say that bothered me, along with the combination of the anger and holding back. It just doesn't suit me. See, my mother was in an abusive situation with my father and I didn't want that for me."

"If you're afraid he's holding back, you need to tell him. Life is crazy, Lauren, because even after he explains, you'll never really know if he's telling the truth."

"I understand that, and I don't want to wonder if he's telling the truth or if he's telling me a lie."

"Lauren, a marriage should be based on trust. If you can't trust the person, then you shouldn't get married."

Lauren stood. "I know, and that's why I'm not getting married."

Ivy reached out to Lauren. "You know I didn't say anything because I felt it was his responsibility to tell you."

"It was his place to tell me. If I hadn't heard him say it myself, he would have never told me."

Ivy got up from the sofa and walked over to her desk. She pulled up Lauren's file on her computer and also retrieved her notebook which had notes concerning things she had put together for the wedding next Friday.

"Lauren, come over here and have a seat." Ivy told her, as she scrolled through the file. "I'm trying to see if there is anything that we can get your money back on. Most wedding items are non-refundable."

Lauren reached over and placed her hand on the desk. "Ivy, I read the contract and the fine print. I already know I can't get my money back, so I don't care. It wasn't mine anyway, it was Randall's."

Ivy suppressed a laugh. She simply said, "Okay. I'm not sure what we can do with your dresses and supplies, but I'll discuss things with Jonathan and my sisters and see what we can come up with."

"I'll have to call everyone on the list to let them know the wedding has been cancelled," Lauren said.

"If you want to avoid a lot of questions, we can do that for you here."

Lauren placed her hand over her chest. "Would you? I don't mind paying for the service."

Ivy shook her head. "There is no need for that, this one is on the house." Ivy pulled up the guest list. "You provided numbers already. We're good."

Lauren stood up and went around to the other side of the desk. "I think I'm getting off cheap, because it would cost me a lot more if I married the wrong man."

Ivy stood as well when Lauren reached out to hug her. "Thank you so much for everything you've done for me."

"It was a pleasure working with you, Lauren. I hope everything that comes your way starting today is a blessing to your life."

"Thank you," Lauren said, stepping back. She walked back over to the chair and picked up her purse. "I feel much better. I wish you much success in all your business ventures." She headed for the door.

Ivy watched Lauren walk out of the door. Despite the way Randall had treated her, Ivy didn't want Lauren to be victimized by her experience with him.

She hoped Lauren would meet someone that would make her happy.

Ivy blew out a big breath, relieved that part was over. Now all she had to do was find a bride and groom for the orphaned wedding.

CHAPTER 22

"Baby, it's not your fault," Jonathan said to Ivy when she called him. He didn't want her to take the burden of what happened between Randall and Lauren upon herself.

"I know, but I feel so bad."

"There's no reason to. If you ask me, the whole situation was stupid from the start. I don't understand why he wasn't honest with the woman from the beginning."

"I'm not being sympathetic toward Randall, I was just thinking about how excited she was about getting married."

"You didn't feel that way after we got married, but aren't you happy about it now?"

After hearing no response, Jonathan knew he'd struck a nerve.

"Ivy, tell me something."

"Yes," she answered quietly.

He could barely hear her. He knew she was nervous.

"Have you thought seriously about what I said the other night?"

"No, I haven't. I'm enjoying us getting to know each other."

"I am, too, but I think it's time for us to seriously think about how we're going to spend the rest of our lives.

Are we going to stay together, or are we going to get an annulment?"

Silence.

"Hello?"

"I'm still here," Ivy said.

"Ivy, don't get quiet on me or feel down about it. All I'm saying is that it's time to think about it. You already know where I stand."

"Yes, I do."

"Good, because I'm not going to mess up what I have with you like Randall did. He didn't handle his business, so now he's alone. I don't want to be that man."

Ivy was breathing hard. "I hear what you're saying, and I promise to seriously think about it."

"Did you want to go out to eat tonight or did you want to stay in?" Jonathan changed the subject. He realized that the day must have been hard for Ivy, but he wanted her to worry about their lives and not someone else's.

"I think I'm going to cook. I'll see you later," she said.

"Tonight," Jonathan said, then waited until she hung up the phone. He stared at the blinking cursor on his computer screen as he pondered his next move in sealing his fate with Ivy.

Jonathan didn't hear his brother when he came into the office.

"Jon," Marc yelled.

Jonathan jumped at the sight of Marc coming toward him.

"Man, you scared me."

Marc took a seat. "What were you thinking about?"

"Ivy Hart just called to tell me that Lauren Kabins cancelled her wedding."

Marc leaned forward, placing his elbows on his knees. "After all the extra charges that had to be paid for rush orders and supplies we've done, now she's not getting married." He shook his head.

"These people don't know what they want to do. They shouldn't start planning their wedding until they've been engaged for at least a year."

Jonathan interrupted. "Okay, you can get off your soap box, bruh. This young lady had some extenuating circumstances."

"I know. The dude she was marrying used to be Ivy's boyfriend back in the day. I know all about it, Rosie told me."

Now Jonathan understood why Ivy didn't want her sisters to know about their marriage. They talked too much.

"Lauren didn't cancel because of Ivy, did she?"

"Hell, no," Jonathan snapped.

Marc held his hands up. "Okay, okay, don't bite my head off. I just asked."

One look at Marc's facial expression and Jonathan knew he'd said the wrong thing.

Marc got up and walked closer to the desk. "What's going on, Jon?"

"Nothing's going on. I just didn't want you to blame Ivy when she didn't have anything to do with that punk not standing up and being a man."

Marc nodded, staring at his brother out of the corner of his eye. "You know what else Rosie told me?"

Jonathan rolled his eyes. "What?"

"You took Ivy out on a date."

"So . . . and . . ."

"What are you holding back from me, little bruh?"

Jonathan got up from his chair and walked back and forth. As always, Marc kept pushing him.

"I think it's cool if you're taking her out. Maybe that's why her attitude has changed. She doesn't seem as uptight as she used to be. I always told Rosie that all her sister needed was the right man to love her."

Jonathan stopped and stared at Marc.

Marc dropped his head. "Don't tell me that you're in love with her." He walked over to the door and back over to the desk, shaking his head the whole time. "Man," he whispered, continuing to move his head from side to side.

Jonathan was still standing in the same spot. "So what if I am in love with her?"

Marc stopped in front of Jonathan. "Don't get me wrong, I think love is a beautiful thing, but with Ivy? I don't know, man. You better be careful, you might get hurt."

It was rare that Jonathan got angry with his brother, but Marc had pissed him off. He walked closer to him. "Remember that time you told me that you would take care of your Mrs. Damon? Well, I can take care of mine."

As soon as the words came out Jonathan regretted them. He'd lost control and blurted out the very thing Ivy wanted to keep secret.

"You married her," Marc said in astonishment.

Jonathan ran over to the door and closed it. He didn't want anyone else in the building to hear them.

Dropping in a chair, he ignored his brother's remarks. It was obvious by the expression on his face that Marc didn't see that one coming.

"When?" Marc yelled, pacing the floor. "Man, I can't believe you got married and didn't tell anybody." He shook his head.

Marc took his seat and they both sat silently.

Time passed quickly and Jonathan knew his brother wasn't finished with the conversation, so he decided to speak first. "I know what you're thinking."

Marc's eyes didn't move from his brother's. "You do, huh? Well then, what am I thinking?"

"I'm a grown man, Marc. I can do whatever I want. It's my marriage, my life and my wife."

"Wrong. I'm thinking that you've done some dumb stuff in the past, but this one . . ." He shook his finger in the air all the while shaking his head. "How did you pull it off? When did you marry Ivy?"

"In Vegas."

Marc looked toward the ceiling. "Back in January?"

Jonathan nodded his answer.

"You've been married to her for almost two months. Her sisters don't know, do they?" Marc jumped up and walked in the opposite direction. "Of course they don't, because Rosie would have told me."

Jonathan had heard enough. It was time that he calmed his brother down and swore him to secrecy.

"Look, Marc, I need you to keep this under your hat."

"Why all the secrecy, Jon?" Marc asked, releasing an aggravated sigh.

"I'm not going into all of that. I just need you to do this for me," Jonathan pleaded.

Marc gave Jonathan a puzzled stare, but then agreed to keep quiet. He opened his mouth to say something else, but Jonathan stopped him.

"Don't say another word about the situation. You never heard me say anything about being married to Ivy. I promise when the time comes, we'll handle the family."

"Man, I hope everything works out. I'm only concerned about your feelings."

"Don't be. I've got this."

Marc walked over to the door and opened it before he said, "I hope so," before leaving the room.

Jonathan hoped his brother didn't hear him say, "Me, too."

❧

Ivy called an urgent meeting in her office with her sisters so they could get some ideas about what to do with Lauren's wedding supplies.

Lili walked in the room last.

"What took you so long?" Rose asked.

"I was busy." She leaned against the wall and crossed her ankles.

"Lauren cancelled her wedding," Ivy said.

Violet's mouth dropped open. "Wow, I was just about to call her to let her know that her dress came in this afternoon."

"Looks like home girl won't be wearing it," Lili said.

"Unfortunately, Lili, you're right," Ivy said, flipping the pages of a notepad she'd been writing in.

"I've made a list of everything we'd done for her. The only thing we can't donate and use for another client would be the invitations."

"If we were to give this wedding away, would the bride need to buy anything?" Rose asked.

"Depending on her size, she would have to buy a dress. Lauren was petite, I think I ordered a size four," Violet said.

"Do we even have a bride that size that hasn't ordered her dress?" Lili asked Violet.

"I'll have to check and see."

"I'm not ever getting married, so you can't even give it to me to put up for later." She laughed.

"Vee, I might know someone," Rose said, her voice filled with excitement.

Ivy raised her brows and gave her a smile in return. "I know where you're going with this Rosie."

Lili frowned. "Well, fill us in. We have no clue what you guys are talking about."

"Did you know that Gwen was engaged?" Rose asked.

Lili threw her hand forward. "Girl, that's old news. Gwen's been engaged for more than a year."

The rest of the sisters looked astonished.

Ivy playfully pushed Lili. "Why didn't you say anything to us about it? You blab about everything else."

"She didn't tell me, her mother did."

Rose smiled. "Mrs. Clark?"

"Yep, she called and asked me if I would bake the wedding cake. She was purchasing it as a gift since Gwen didn't have the money."

Ivy picked up the phone. "Let's get her in here. We need to talk to her."

Violet pressed the button to hang up the call.

"Why did you do that, Violet?" Ivy asked.

"If she wanted us to know, don't you think she would have told us all? You guys keep forgetting this isn't our business."

Ivy laid her hand on the phone. "I'm sorry, Violet, but I want to do this for her. If anybody deserves this, it's Gwen."

Before Ivy lifted the receiver again, she asked the rest of her sisters, "Are we all on the same page?"

They all nodded, yes.

Ivy asked Gwen to come into her office. Once she arrived, Ivy asked, "Gwen, have you and your fiancée picked a wedding date?"

A surprised expression covered Gwen's nut brown face. She dropped her head. "I didn't want you guys to treat me as a charity case. I wanted to pay for my wedding like any other customer."

"Umph," Lili said. "Girl, if I worked at a place like this and I had a good relationship with my boss, I'd be trying to get everything I could for free."

"You would," Ivy added.

They all laughed.

Clearing her throat, Ivy's playful attitude disappeared.

Violet placed her hand on Gwen's shoulder. "We wouldn't think of you as a charity case. We'd love to help you. And that's why you're here today."

"Yes, one of our clients cancelled her wedding. She told me to give her items to a bride that needed it. You not only need it, but you deserve it," Rose said proudly.

"Why don't we go over everything being offered to you, Gwen? You don't have to take anything you don't want," Ivy said.

"Yeah, especially those ugly lime green and peach bridesmaid's dresses," Lili added.

Violet shook her head. "They actually are really lovely. They came in today, but there are only three dresses."

"How many bridesmaids do you have?" Ivy asked.

"I only have one, my sister Shauna."

Ivy noticed Gwen's demeanor had changed. She figured all of this was overwhelming, so she wanted to slow down the pace of the meeting.

"Listen Gwen, we got so excited about being able to do this, we didn't even ask you if you were interested."

Tears were rolling down Gwen's face. Lili went and picked up the open box of tissue that sat on Ivy's credenza and dropped it in her lap. "Girl, you better say something quick."

Gwen looked at each person one by one before she said, "Are you sure you want to do this for me? I know you have others that you could give these things to."

The sisters looked at each other then back at Gwen. They all responded together: "We're sure."

"Then I'm sure," Gwen said, hugging Violet.

She embraced everyone before Ivy spoke again. "Gwen, there is only one catch to this whole situation."

Gwen's eyes widened filled with tears. "What's that?"

Ivy leaned forward. "You have to get married next Friday night."

"I don't think Anthony will care. He's wanted to get married at the courthouse over a year, but had been patient because I wanted to have something special."

Ivy pulled Gwen to her side. "Well, sweetheart, you've finally got your something special."

There was a spirit of joy and peace that permeated the room. Ivy was once again excited about being able to make another bride's dreams come true. They sat down and went through every detail and gathered the other ideas Gwen had for her special day; next week, she would be getting married at Magic Moments.

Ivy almost missed the deadline for her column because she was trying to finalize everything for Gwen's candlelight wedding and reception. Now that Gwen had gotten married and was off on her honeymoon, she could e-mail it to her editor.

Everyone seemed to be pleased with the romantic and heartfelt ceremony. Ivy had put together a lot of weddings, so she'd heard all the things that were said at the ceremony before, but the words the minister spoke to Gwen and Anthony really touched her heart. The sheer happiness on the couples faces was extraordinary. Once Gwen made it to the altar, it appeared that they were the only two people in the room.

Ivy had been so caught up in the moment that she didn't care that Jonathan stood in the back with her and caught her hand when the minister started the vows. Everyone had done their job well and now it was on to the next bride.

"Vee," Rose said when she walked into the room.

Ivy looked up from her computer. "Hey, Rosie."

"Gwen made a beautiful bride, didn't she?" Rose sat down in front of Ivy.

"Everything was just lovely. Now, I've got to get caught up. It's time to tape the next couple for the show." Ivy said.

"When will they air them?"

"In the fall. They'll alternate between the three cities. So one Sunday it will be me, the next, the New York planner and then the L.A. planner."

"I'm excited. I can't wait to see it."

"How's it going answering phones?"

"The temp they sent over from the agency is doing an okay job. She's fascinated with the wedding business, so I think if we can get her to focus she'll do a good job."

"Most women, whether they admit it or not, love weddings and all that they represent," Ivy said.

"I came down here to invite you over to my house for dinner on Friday night. Marc is going to make us a fabulous meal."

"Sure, Rosie, I'll be there."

Rose stood up and said, "Now that you and Jonathan have gotten cozy, I don't have to tell you that he's going to be there, too."

Ivy chuckled. "No, you don't. I'm okay with him being there, Rosie."

"I'm so glad you're starting to socialize with us more."

"Marc's a great cook, and we had a lot of fun that night we went skating," Ivy replied.

"I'm going to check on our temp." Rose disappeared through the door.

Ivy picked up the phone and called Violet.

"Yes, ma'am," Violet said when she picked up.

"Are you going over to Rosie's Friday night for dinner?"

"I'll be there. You know I love Marc's cooking, especially when he does those fancy dishes."

Ivy smiled. "I said the same thing. I wonder who else is going to be at the party."

"She said she was inviting everybody. We'll just have to wait and see."

Violet hesitated before she spoke again. "Vee, how are you doing sorting out your feelings for Jonathan?"

"You know he wants us to live together now."

"And . . ."

"I don't know, Violet. I'm just as confused as I was before."

"But you said that you loved him."

"I do, I really do, but . . ."

"But, you don't trust him."

"I trust him," Ivy said before releasing a groan. "I don't know."

"I won't badger you about it. You know how you feel about him. Just keep on doing what you're doing, taking things one step at a time."

CHAPTER 23

It was Friday already and another week had come and gone. Ivy had completed her last taping with the second couple and now she was on the home stretch. She was given the last portfolio and would meet with the final couple, Ryan Curtis and Keisha Marshall, next week.

Business had picked up for the upcoming summer and fall wedding season.

She and Jonathan continued to enjoy each other's company, laughing and talking about their favorite music, childhood memories and movies. She was surprised when he said that the movie *The Best Man* was his all time favorite with *Love and Basketball* coming in a close second. Both movies were in her top five.

They made love with such passion that she was unable to put her feelings into words.

Ivy took a quick shower and then walked into her closet to find something to wear for the evening. She laughed at Rose when she called and asked Ivy to wear red to the dinner party. Ivy knew that red was Rose's favorite color, so she obliged. She carefully chose a red three-piece pants suit. It had strips of satin and lace appliqué, beads and gems on the collar, cuffs and the camisole. She paired it with her diamond stud earrings and red oxford pumps.

Admiring herself in the mirror, she heard the doorbell. She hurried to the door.

"Look at my baby," Jonathan said, smiling brightly, as he walked into the condo.

Ivy, feeling playful, modeled the outfit for him.

Jonathan put two fingers in his mouth, whistling. "You really dressed up, didn't you?" He pulled her to him.

Ivy stepped back and went to the closet to retrieve her coat. "Rosie called and asked me to wear red."

She looked over at him. "You're not shortstopping." Ivy loved the way his red shirt complimented the black pinstriped pants and vest.

Placing a kiss on his lips, she said, "I guess they're going to pull out their best china."

Jonathan chuckled. "Yeah, I guess. When my brother gets in the mood to cook, he goes all out. Did she tell you what was on the menu?"

"No, she just said dress up and prepare to have a good time."

Jonathan took the coat from her. "Well, let me help you with that and we can get this party started."

＊⟶

There were lots of cars lining the driveway and parked on the street at Rose and Marc's house.

Ivy pointed. "My mom and dad are here."

"I see Uncle Isaiah's car here, too," Jonathan said.

Jonathan found a parking space along the curb in front of Violet's late model Lexus.

They got out of the car and walked the short distance to the house. As they went up the sidewalk to the front door, Ivy noticed that Rose had found a way to redecorate the outside of the house with lights that illuminated the pathway. She always loved the way Rose added her personal touch to her home.

Jonathan rang the bell. When Marc opened the door Ivy thought he gave her a funny look when they exchanged hellos. She shrugged it off as her imagination and promised herself that she wouldn't be paranoid. This party wasn't for her, it was for Rose.

Rose and Marc had lived in the home for two years. Each and every time Ivy visited her sister, she saw something different. When they walked into the living room, she noticed that Rose had placed four gorgeous new paintings on the wall. Ivy was admiring them when Rose came over to her.

"Girl, you know you sharp," Rose said to Ivy before giving Jonathan a hug.

"Look at you, you are simply glowing," Ivy said, pulling her sister to her.

Rose stepped back and curtsied. "Why, thank you so much ma'am," she said playfully, turning so Ivy could see the red loose-fitting jacket dress with print duster trimmed in white satin. She stuck her leg out so that Ivy could see the slits on the sides.

Ivy looked up again at the paintings. "Where did you get these? I love the abstract shapes."

"Would you believe I found them at an estate sale?"

"Really?"

"Yeah, and we paid about twenty dollars apiece for them," Rose said, walking away, and then stopping right in front of the threshold of the door.

"Everybody's in the family room," Rose announced.

Ivy and Jonathan walked into the spacious room. Her parents and the Damons were sitting on the large leather pit-style set listening to music. There was a big-screen television, entertainment center and lots of family photos on the wall.

"Hey, everybody," she said, waving her hand. Jonathan walked in behind her and did the same. He walked over to properly greet his aunt and uncle while Ivy went to speak to her parents. She was surprised to see her mother holding a wine glass.

"Mom, what are you drinking?" Ivy asked, giving her a hug.

After squeezing her daughter, Louvenia handed Ivy the glass. "Moscato, I think," she said with uncertainty. "Lili gave that to me. She knows I don't drink, but she said that Rosie wanted everyone to have a glass."

"Oh," Ivy said. She moved around to the other side to place a kiss on her father's cheek. "Hey, Daddy."

"How's my baby girl?"

"Good." She patted her mother's knee. "You guys look nice in your matching red outfits."

Andrew glanced over at Louvenia. "Your mother made me wear this. You know I hate red."

Louvenia turned up her nose and shook her head at her husband's statement.

"Where are Lili and Violet?" Ivy asked.

Andrew Hart crossed his legs at the ankle. "They are helping Marc in the kitchen."

Ivy went over to speak to the Damons, and then she left to look for her sisters.

Walking through the dining room area, she stopped to inspect the beautiful table settings. A crinkled silk cloth covered the formal dining room table which seated eight with matching chair covers. It was adorned with one continuous centerpiece of garden and spray roses, kaleidoscope phalaenopsis orchids and sweet pea. Another smaller table had been decorated in the same manner.

Ivy could do nothing but smile. She walked to the kitchen where she found Violet.

"Wow, this is going to be some kind of party," Ivy said to Violet as she ladled the soup into the dish.

"It smells good in here." She walked closer to Violet. "You better be careful not to ruin your outfit." Ivy pulled the apron her sister wore up further around her neck and retied it so it would cover her entire front.

"Thanks, Vee. I'm trying not to just sit down and serve myself some of this soup."

Ivy peeked into the pot that was on the stove. "It looks like clam chowder."

"It is, and mmmm, it smells so good."

"You need any help?"

Violet looked around. "No, I don't think so, Marc only asked me to put the soup in the tureen, and he'll take care of the rest."

Ivy scanned the kitchen. "Where is Lili?"

"She'll be back, she said that the cake got messed up or something and she didn't bring any of her supplies."

"That girl." Ivy shook her head. "Well, if you don't need any help, I'm going back to the family room."

Violet picked up a clean towel and wiped her hands off. Placing the ladle inside the bowl, she put the lid on it. "I'm going with you," she said, removing the apron and laying it on the back of the chair.

"Where's Jonathan?" Violet asked.

"He's around here somewhere. When I left, he was talking to his aunt and uncle," Ivy replied as they approached the room.

"Is the food ready yet?" Andrew asked.

"Not just yet, Daddy," Ivy answered. She sat down on the other side of her parents on the couch.

"It should be in a minute, though," Violet said.

They waited for the host and hostess to come into the room.

Finally, Rose and Marc both entered the room together. Rose stepped forward and addressed everyone. Marc came to stand next to her, and then pulled her to his side.

"Marc and I asked you all to come over this evening because we have something to tell you."

Everyone sat straight up in their seats.

Rose looked up at Marc, tears brimming in her eyes. Marc bent to kiss her, before Andrew yelled out, "Will you tell us already?"

Isaiah said, "Don't keep us in suspense."

"We're having a baby," Marc said quickly.

Excitement filled the room as the grandparents-to-be surrounded the happy couple. Ivy didn't know why her heart sank. It definitely wasn't because she was jealous of Rose. She understood how badly Rose wanted to be a mother, and this news was her dream come true.

Until recently, she never even thought about being a mother. She'd left all those thoughts behind after her accident. It only occurred to Ivy at that moment: maybe she couldn't have any children.

Jonathan came over to her. "Baby, why don't we go out on the deck for a minute?" He held out his hand to her.

Ivy looked up at him and placed her hand in his. The concern he showed for her was one of the reasons she loved him. As they passed Marc and Rose, Ivy stopped.

Her eyes widened when she hugged her sister and Rose whispered, "You told me to stop worrying, and I did."

When she said those words, tears spilled down Ivy's cheeks. She was truly happy for Rose.

They hugged again and Ivy could see Rose's tears. Ivy retreated and said, "I'm going to be Auntie Vee." She smiled and waited for Jonathan to give them his congratulations.

Ivy and Jonathan walked through the dining area into the kitchen. They walked to the back, he slid the door open enough for them to step out on the deck.

"It's chilly out here," Ivy said, rubbing her arms.

Jonathan invited her into his open arms. "Come here, baby." He held her close to him, whispering, "We'll go back inside in a minute. I saw the sad expression on your face when Rose made her announcement and thought maybe you needed some air." He released her.

Looking into her eyes he asked, "You want to be a mother, too, don't you?"

"I hadn't thought about being a mom in a very long time. I'm not sure what triggered it, but lately . . ." Her voice trailed off.

Jonathan lifted her chin, so that he could look into her eyes. "It's okay to say it, baby."

Tears brimming, she finally said, "I want to be a mommy."

Jonathan hugged her again. "I know you do, and you will."

Curving his arm around her shoulders, he held her to his side. "Come on, let's get inside. I don't want you to catch a cold."

They walked back inside to join the rest of the family in the celebration.

"Where did you guys slip off to?" Violet asked Ivy when she and Jonathan returned.

"I just needed to get some air, and Jonathan went with me."

Jonathan touched her elbow. "Baby, I'm going to help Marc out in the kitchen."

Ivy nodded.

Violet responded by raising her eyebrow. Ivy ignored the look and asked, "Where's Lili?"

Violet shrugged.

Ivy checked her watch. "She's been gone a long time."

"Knowing Lili, she might have remade the cake or something," Violet said.

Rose came over to where they were standing. "Aww, mommy," Violet said, reaching for Rose.

"How are you feeling?" Ivy asked, rubbing Rose's back as she and Violet hugged each other.

"I feel great today, but I felt tired all the time for the last two weeks. I thought it was because we had been so busy, but when I got up the other morning and the room was spinning like I'd just got off a Ferris wheel, I started paying more attention. I went to the doctor, took a blood test and they told me that I was pregnant." Rose could barely get it out without crying.

Ivy hugged her. "I'm so happy for you. You're going to make a great mom."

"Where is Lili?" their mother asked.

"That seems to be the question of the hour," Violet said.

"We need to eat soon, because you know how your father is when he's really hungry."

"Come on, let's eat," Rose said, walking toward the doorway. "We don't have to wait for Lili, she'll get something when she comes in," Rose said.

Everyone followed her to the dining room.

Jonathan entered the kitchen, where Marc was working to get the food on the platters.

"Man, have you ever seen Aunt Rachel cry like that before?" Jonathan asked.

"No, and it looked like Unc shed a few of his own."

Jonathan's eyes got big. "He'd never admit to it."

"For sho," Marc commented as he put the rice pilaf on a long white dish.

Jonathan grabbed a set of oven mitts and removed the steaks from the broiler. He placed the tray on the stove so the meat could sit and the juices redistribute themselves. "Are you excited about the baby?" he asked his brother.

Marc stopped what he was doing. "Man, I feel like I'm ten feet tall. I really can't explain how I feel about it. You'll understand once you and Ivy have kids."

"Maybe, I don't know. She got really emotional about the baby announcement, so I took her out on the deck and we talked for a bit."

Marc was ready to take his plate out of the room. "So it looks like the marriage is working out for you two?"

Jonathan beamed with pride. "We are solid. I told her that we would be fine."

"You really do love her. I can see it now. The way your eyes sparkle when you talk about her. How the tone of your voice changes when you say her name."

Marc raised his hand. "Many blessings to y'all, man." They slapped each other a high five.

Jonathan picked up his platter and Marc lifted his from the table. Neither of them saw Lili when she came in through the side door of the kitchen. She'd heard their whole conversation.

"Well, it's about time you came back," Rose told Lili when she walked into the dining room.

Lili waved. "Evening, everybody."

Leaning over, Lili whispered in Rose's ear. "Come upstairs with me. I need to tell you something."

Rose looked puzzled. "What is it?"

"Just come upstairs."

"But we're getting ready to eat and I'm already nauseous."

"It won't take long, I promise."

Rose watched as her guests took their seats at the table to enjoy the feast that Marc had prepared. They dined on crab cakes and scallops for the hors d'oeuvres, then clam chowder. He served a gourmet meal of delicious steak and tender salmon while she and Lili were in her bedroom upstairs.

CHAPTER 24

As soon as they entered her bedroom, Rose closed the door and turned to Lili. "What have you done?" she whispered.

Lili frowned. "Me? What have I done? Not a thing, it's your other sister."

It was Rose's turn to frown. "Stop it, Lili."

"No, really, Vee is the one who's in the hot seat this time."

"Vee? What did she do?"

Lili put her hands on her hips and sashayed over to the dresser and stared at herself in the mirror.

"Spill it, Lili. I know you didn't bring me up here to play a game of dress-up. So tell me what you were told or what you heard. I know it was either one or the two."

"Vee got married."

Rose squinted, trying to process the information she'd just been given. "Wherever you heard that, it can't be right. Don't you think we would have known if she'd gotten married?" Rose started walking back and forth in front of the door. "Who would she get married to? She just started dating Jonathan."

Rose stared at Lili, who stood silently.

Slowly, Rose said, "Jonathan?"

Lili nodded slowly.

Rose moved purposefully over to Lili and grabbed her arm. "Let's go," she said, anger in her tone, as she dragged her sister out of the room.

"Where are we going?" Lili asked, struggling to remove herself from her sister's grip.

"You'll see in a minute." They walked swiftly down the stairs, and as soon as they walked into the dining room, Rose pushed Lili in front of her. "I want you to tell them what you just told me."

Lili stepped back, but Rose just pushed her forward again.

Louvenia glared at both her daughters before saying, "Will one of you please tell us so that we can eat? We have been waiting long enough; the food is going to get cold."

Lili stared at Ivy, her face turned up. Then she looked at Jonathan before glancing at her parents.

Hunching her shoulders, she said, "We've got something else to celebrate."

Louvenia fell back against her chair. "Please don't tell me you're pregnant, too."

Lili waved her right hand vigorously. "No, no, nothing like that, Mother." She glanced at every person sitting at the table one by one. "You could congratulate me, though."

"Baby girl, you are stalling," Andrew said, pointing his fork at her.

Lili turned to Rose and said, "Okay, congratulations to me, I'm going to be an aunt and I found out I got a new brother-in-law, all in the same day."

Ivy scowled. Throwing her napkin on the floor, she pushed her chair back in a hurry and yanked her arm back when Jonathan tried to stop her.

She walked directly over to Lili. "Who told you?" Her nostrils flared. "I have told you that your mouth is going to get you into trouble one day. Well, today is the day."

Jonathan jumped up from his seat as their parents looked on in amazement. Once again Ivy snatched her hand back when he tried to catch her hand. "I want to explain what happened," he said.

Louvenia stood to her feet. "Somebody better explain, and quick."

Ivy's anger was apparent. She turned to Jonathan and yelled, "You had no right to tell my business. I wanted to tell my parents, and you took away that right." Jonathan reached out to her and she turned her back.

Marc got up from his seat and went to her. "Ivy, don't blame Jonathan, it was my fault. Lili must have been in the kitchen listening to our conversation earlier."

Ivy twisted her head to the side, but her back stayed to Jonathan. "I don't care if it was your fault. He had to be the one to tell you."

Marc looked down at his hands. "He didn't actually tell me, Ivy. I guessed."

She turned to face him. "He didn't deny it. Did he?"

"No, he didn't, but he was defending you, and I guess it just slipped out."

Jonathan hadn't moved from where he was standing. He attempted one last time to reach out to Ivy. This time he touched her shoulder. "Can we talk about this in private?"

Ivy rolled her eyes and turned to face him. "In private? For what? All you're going to do is put our business out on the streets anyway. What good would it do if we were in a room all by ourselves?"

Silently, Ivy walked from the room and got her coat. Once she was at the door, she remembered she came with Jonathan. She walked back in the room and beckoned for Violet.

"Will you take me home? I forgot I didn't drive my car."

Jonathan stepped over to her. "I'll take you home. We can talk on the way."

Ivy threw her left hand in his face. "I'm done talking to you." She looked at her sister for an answer.

Violet got up from her chair and retrieved her coat.

Rose went to Marc and asked, "How long have you known Vee and Jonathan were married?"

"Not long."

"And you didn't tell me?"

Marc pulled Rose into his arms and kissed her. "We'll talk about this later. Right now I need to see about my brother."

On the way to Ivy's condo, the only voice that could be heard was the disc jockey on the smooth jazz radio station.

Violet glanced over at Ivy. "Vee, you can't really get mad at him. You told me."

Ivy jerked her head in her sister's direction. "That was different, it was my right."

"It's his marriage, too, so he has equal rights."

"He took mine away when he told his brother."

"Marc said he didn't tell him, he guessed."

"Who gives a damn? We don't care how we get a dollar, ten dimes, four quarters, it all equals a dollar. That's how I feel about this situation." Jonathan's promises of secrecy played over and over in her mind.

"Just drop me off, please, and we don't have to talk about Jonathan Damon ever again in this lifetime."

Trying to reason with Ivy, Violet said, "You don't mean what you're saying. I know you don't, Vee."

Ivy turned to Violet. "I can't trust the man. That was the very reason why I didn't want to get involved in the first place."

Violet pulled up in front of Ivy's condo. "I don't understand what you're saying."

"Violet, you know better than I do that trust is the foundation of a relationship."

Violet carefully reached over and patted Ivy on the thigh. "Vee, trust is very important, but I think love and trust go hand-in-hand. And I don't think you'd be this upset if you didn't deeply love Jonathan."

"I'll get over it." Ivy reached for the handle to open her door.

As she was getting out, she heard Violet ask, "Do you want me to stay for a while?"

"No, I'll be fine." Ivy slammed the door and went into her house.

Standing in front of the window in the den, Jonathan attempted to smile, but his heart was broken. He wanted to be angry at Lili, his brother and everybody else, but the truth of the matter was that he betrayed her trust. He wanted to shout to anyone who would listen that Ivy Hart was indeed his wife. But after she'd explained to him her past and how hurt she had been, he understood why she wanted to sort things out.

He felt a hand on his shoulder. Turning around slowly, he faced his Aunt Rachel.

Rachel embraced him and whispered in his ear, "Things will work out. You'll see."

Jonathan retreated. "I'm not going to let her go, Auntie."

She rubbed his back. "That's right, baby, you fight for your wife. If you think she's worth it and your love can sustain this, then fight."

"I'm going to take your uncle home, but once you've calmed down and can think straight, I want you to come by the house. I want to give something to you."

Jonathan only nodded and bent to receive the kiss she placed on his forehead.

It was time for him to go as well. He'd decided not to go over to Ivy's house tonight, but, bright and early in the morning, he'd be ringing her bell.

As he walked to the coat closet to retrieve his jacket, Lili approached him.

"I'm sorry, Jonathan. I didn't know Vee would react that way."

Jonathan turned around. "Yes, you did, Lili. We know how private your sister is and that she wouldn't have wanted that information blurted out like that."

Lili dropped her head.

Jonathan rested his hand on her shoulder. "This should be a lesson to you. You just can't go around telling other people's business, especially when it's not your story to tell."

With that, he put his coat on and left her standing there alone.

Jonathan didn't speak to anyone else; he walked out the door, climbed into his truck and left.

CHAPTER 25

Ivy's phone had rung so much in the last twenty-four hours that she turned the ringer off. Each time she saw Jonathan's number, she'd delete his voicemails unheard. She didn't want to explain, answer any questions or talk to anyone, period. She pulled out her portfolio and tried to concentrate on the tasks she must complete next week, but she couldn't. Each time she attempted to read the couple's bio, her eyes would get so watery that she couldn't see.

Laying the notebook aside, she slid down under the covers of her bed and closed her eyes. She didn't usually allow things to get her so depressed that she was confined to her bed, but she didn't have the energy to do anything else.

Closing her eyes, all she could see was Jonathan's dark face. She opened her eyes and shook her head as if the action would get him out of her head.

The doorbell rang and Ivy didn't move. It had to either be one of her sisters or Jonathan, and she didn't want to see any of them. She wanted to be alone so she could think things through.

There was no way she could function as a business-woman with her head all messed up.

Pushing herself out of the bed, she went to the drawer to get clean underclothes. Maybe if she stood in the shower, she could muster up some energy.

Opening the drawer, she saw the white envelope lying on top.

Tears immediately filled her eyes. She picked up the flimsy paper, walked back over to the bed and flopped down. Shoulders slumped, head bowed, she covered it with her hand and sat quietly for a while. After exhaling, she opened the envelope and pulled out their wedding picture.

Tracing his face in the photo, she thought that they were strangers to each other when it was taken. Now, she had to resign herself to the fact that there was no getting around loving Jonathan. As badly as he hurt her, she loved him; but what if he told her other secret?

A look of horror showed on Ivy's face. She didn't want to think about the aftermath if that bombshell were revealed. Even though it was an accident, she never told anyone in her family about her pregnancy, not even Violet.

The single person she bared her soul to was the one who betrayed her. Placing the picture back inside, she didn't dare remove anything else from the pouch. She was determined now more than ever to finish her filming schedule and get out to Vegas to get an annulment.

The final taping of Ivy's show was over, and she was elated. She didn't think she could continue to act bright and cheery when she was sad and miserable. The feeling of loss plagued her. She could barely function normally; everything she did reminded her of Jonathan. She was relieved that they didn't have any meetings scheduled any time soon.

It had been three days since she'd spoken to him or her sister Lili. Even though her mother reminded her that she wasn't raised to stop speaking to her sister, Ivy didn't feel it was her responsibility to come to apologize first. Lili was the blabbermouth; she should be the one to apologize.

Driving to the office, she heard the ring tone signaling she had a call. With her Bluetooth securely in her ear, she answered.

"Ivy Hart speaking."

"Vee, where are you?"

"Why, Rosie?"

"Because I need to talk to you."

"Are you and the baby okay?"

"Yes, we're fine."

"Is it about the business or a bride?"

"No."

"Well, then, we don't have anything else to talk about."

"Are you coming back to the office?"

"Why?"

Rose groaned. "Okay, Vee. Have it your way."

Ivy ended the call without saying goodbye. She recognized Rose's ploy to find out what time she was coming back to the office so she could possibly have Jonathan there or something.

Ivy turned on her music and relaxed all the way back to the office.

Jonathan had taken the day off from work. He needed to do some soul searching, and he wasn't focused anyway. His brother suggested he take a few days off. He assured Jonathan that his assistant could handle things until he got back.

Jonathan rested in his black leather recliner listening to Sade. After a while, he had to get up and put on something else, because the music was making him feel worse. Being depressed didn't fit him. He couldn't think, rest, share, or anything else when he was sad.

He recognized the fact that for the last three days Ivy hadn't returned his calls or responded to his text messages or e-mails. He just wanted a chance to talk things out as adults.

Each day he would hope against hope that she would give them that chance. When she didn't, he would pull together the courage to keep on believing that tomorrow she would share a conversation with him.

He jumped when his cell phone buzzed. He quickly pulled it from his belt clip, hoping it was Ivy. His heart dropped when he saw the caller was Rachel.

"Hey, Auntie."

"Hey, baby, why don't you come on over here? I really need to talk to you."

"Aunt Rach, I don't want to hear . . ." Rachel interrupted him before he could finish.

"I'll see you in fifteen minutes."

She hung up the phone and Jonathan sat for several minutes more before he decided to leave.

"Come with me," she said as she headed to her bedroom. "Sit over on the bed, son." She lifted the lid of the window seat in her room.

"I wanted it to just be me and you when we had our little talk." She pulled out a gray box and brought it over to the bed.

"Auntie, what is this about? I've got a lot on my mind already, so if either you or Uncle Zeke is ill, please just tell me."

Rachel patted his hand. "Be patient, honey. I just need to find something really important I put in this box," she said, sifting through its contents.

"Do you want me to help you look for it?"

"No, I found it," she said, pulling a sealed envelope from the bottom of the box and handing it to him. She then went back to her chest of drawers, apparently looking for something else.

"Auntie, what are you looking for now?"

"There is something that goes with the letter." She continued searching until she found a small blue velvet box. Returning to the bed, she handed the box to him.

He finally realized that his aunt was giving him a letter and gift from his mother. Ever since Marc had received his letter and gift, he had wondered what his letter would say. But seeing his name on the envelope in

his mother's own handwriting was completely unexpected. She'd been so ill, so it must have taken a lot of
strength and determination to write.

"Go on, sweetheart, open the letter," Rachel urged.

"Why now?" he asked.

"Because it's time," she said, moving away to give him
some privacy.

He ran his index finger along the envelope's flap,
opening it and pulling out a sheet of paper. Unshed tears
stung the back of his eyes.

My sweet baby boy,

*I've asked your Aunt Rachel to hold on to this letter for
you until she felt you were ready to read it. If you're reading
it now, she thinks you're ready.*

*Oh, baby, you've always been so brave. I've never seen
fear in your eyes, and that says a lot for a little boy. You are
such a loving person. I know you're too young to understand
what's going on, but never forget that I'll always love you.*

*You know, it has been said that when we look at our
children, we see a mirror image of ourselves. I wonder, I
really do, if I could be as brave as you. I am sad that I won't
be there to protect you as you grow up, but I know that even
though your father is in pain, he will be there for you.*

*I do feel guilty leaving you and Marc at such tender ages,
but I'm sure that your Aunt Rachel will do her best to love
and nurture you and your brother. I keep thinking, what do
I have to leave you? Will you forget about me? That is why
I decided to write you boys a letter. I wanted to leave some*

lasting words of advice and encouragement in my own words, not just something somebody will tell you.

The best thing Momma can tell you is that forgiveness goes a long way. I hope you and Marc will forgive me for leaving you. Son, when you forgive, it helps you heal as well as helping the person you are forgiving. Live life to the fullest and love just as hard. It's okay to show emotion, and sometimes something or someone will hurt you. Before giving up or walking away, think about forgiving that person and yourself. That way, if you find that the end result is walking away, you'll be able to do so with a clear conscience. I've also asked your aunt to give you a gift to give to your wife someday. It is an heirloom brooch that my momma gave to me. I want you to have it, along with the remembrance of my love and devotion to you.

I know we will all be together again one day.

Yours forever,
Momma

Putting the letter aside, Jonathan picked up the blue box and opened it. Inside on a bed of blue velvet was a diamond brooch.

"Wow," he exclaimed. It was one of the most exquisite pieces of jewelry he'd ever seen.

The delicate piece consisted of pave-set diamonds with a teardrop dangling below a bar at the top. It was accented with an inlay of iridescent pink mother-of-pearl.

Jonathan looked up and saw the tears streaming down Rachel's face.

"Auntie," he said, looking back at the brooch. Overwhelmed, he didn't know what to say.

Rachel pulled Jonathan into her arms. "Sweetie, your momma was in so much pain. One day she told me that she wanted to write to you and Marc before she got to the point where she didn't know her name. You know, from all the medication she was on."

Rachel gently caressed his face. "Right away, I got her paper and a pen so she could put her thoughts down on paper. It was important to her that she say what was in her heart without any interference from anyone, so I left her alone."

"You didn't know what was in the letter?"

"No, she only asked that I give you boys the gifts," Rachel said, getting up and going over to the chest of drawers, where she pulled out another small box and brought it back to the bed.

"See, I have a brooch very similar to the one your mother left you. In fact your Aunt Anna and Aunt Bertha have one, too. The difference is my mother-of-pearl is white, Anna's is yellow and Bertha's is sapphire blue. Our mother gave us each one for our thirteenth birthdays."

After a moment of silence, Jonathan spoke. "She said she wanted me to give it to my wife, but my wife really doesn't want to be my wife. I can't give it to her."

Rachel got up from the bed and stood in front of him. "Jonathan, you still haven't spoken to Ivy yet?" she asked, her voice a mixture of disbelief and concern.

"No."

"Why?"

"I've reached out to her, but she won't respond. I've tried everything. I sent her flowers, I called and emailed her, but she just won't answer me."

"Have you tried talking to her in person?"

"I thought about it."

"Jonathan, I'm not going to ask you when you got married or why you didn't tell us. I want you to be happy, so I think you need to go and talk to her."

Before Jonathan could respond, his uncle entered the room.

"Hey, Johnny, my boy, I saw your car outside. You know you should have told us you were getting married."

Rachel grabbed her husband's hand and pulled him along when it seemed as if he was getting ready to scold Jonathan.

"Come on, I left the tea kettle on the stove."

"I turned it off when I came in," Isaiah said, still waiting and watching Jonathan.

Jonathan dropped his head. "All I can say is I'm sorry I didn't tell you."

Rachel took Isaiah's hand again, and this time he went with her.

Ivy stopped at the receptionist's desk to pick up her mail. Gwen still hadn't come back to work, so she wanted to check up on the receptionist.

"You have six messages, Ms. Hart, and three I transferred to your voicemail," the young woman said.

"Thanks so much, Belinda. I'm going to my office. You know how to buzz me if you need me, right?"

"Yes, I do."

As soon as Ivy walked away, Belinda called her name. "Ms. Hart, I forgot, you had several floral deliveries."

Ivy walked back to the station. "Did you tell Rose? She's the floral designer. I don't handle that."

"No, these were personal flower deliveries for you. I didn't look at the cards, so I can't tell you who sent them."

"Thanks, Belinda." As she strolled down the hall, Ivy could smell the exotic fragrance. Once she got closer, she could see the shadows of about a dozen arrangements through the frosted glass.

Several bouquets of roses sat on the floor just inside the entryway. Beautiful yellow, purple, and pink tulips, snapdragons, and freesia in a glass ginger vase sat on her desk, along with a crystal vase with pink French tulips, oriental lilies, seven pink snapdragons and seven stemmed diamond eucalyptus.

The sender was evident, so there was no need to look at the cards. Jonathan had to have spent a fortune on the flowers, since she did notice that they came from an outside vendor.

Removing several bouquets from her desk so she could work, Ivy tried to pretend that the beauty and fragrance didn't affect her. They were a sweet gesture.

Ivy looked up when she heard a knock on her door.

"Yes, Lili, what do you want?" she asked, continuing her task.

"Vee, we need to talk."

Engrossed in her work, Ivy didn't respond or give Lili her attention.

"We need to talk," Lili repeated, walking into the room.

"About?" Ivy replied, continuing to check her e-mail.

"I keep calling your name and you act as if you need a hearing aid. I know you're trying to ignore me, but I'm not going away," Lili said, her hand on her hip.

"I'm not ignoring you, Lili. I did ask what you wanted," Ivy replied, looking up from her paper to face her sister.

"Vee, I'm sorry for what happened."

"You're always sorry once you get in trouble," Ivy said, frowning.

"I didn't know you would get so angry."

"I don't have time for your foolishness. If you have something worth saying, out with it so we can get back to work."

"Look, I'm saying it," Lili said, dropping into the chair.

"I not only hurt you, but Jonathan is really messed up. I didn't mean to do that."

Ivy glared at her sister. She could hear the remorse in her voice. Ivy bent forward. "We all have to grow up some time, Lili. I think it's time that you did."

Lili jumped to her feet. "I know, I know. When I overheard them talking about you and Jonathan being married, I couldn't help myself."

"My marrying Jonathan was nobody's business." Ivy got up from her seat and walked around the desk. "I had my reasons for not telling anyone about the marriage."

Stepping forward, Lili reached out to touch Ivy's arm. "Why would you do that?"

Ivy stared at Lili. "I know you don't think I'm going to tell you."

They both laughed, before Lili said, "You got me. I deserved that one."

Ivy couldn't stay mad at Lili, so she hugged her. "You better learn how to keep your mouth shut. You just can't go around telling other people's business." She released her and said, "Somebody could get hurt."

"Somebody did get hurt, and that was the last thing I wanted," Lili said, nodding in agreement.

She headed for the door, then stopped and said, "I'll check you later."

Holding up her hand to stop her, Ivy said, "Please take a couple bouquets of flowers with you."

"He really wants you back, huh."

"Lili," Ivy said, in a warning tone of voice.

Lili grabbed two bouquets of roses. "Okay, okay, I'm outta here."

After Lili left, Ivy looked around the room and still felt she was in a flower garden.

CHAPTER 26

Jonathan stood in front of his armoire gazing at the beautiful brooch his mother had left him. The intricate piece of jewelry would look stunning pinned on one of Ivy's business suits. He'd cherish the gift for the rest of his life.

With the drawer opened, he contemplated what to do about his situation with Ivy. He'd told himself that he was doing the right thing by giving her space and that she would call as soon as she was ready, just like she did the last time.

His heart didn't believe that, because this situation was altogether different. The first time they barely knew each other, so it was understandable that she needed time to sort things out. But now that he knew her heart, discussing the situation was the solution.

Fear of rejection and abandonment were the culprits behind Ivy's tirade. Sure, he should not have blurted out his business, but he wasn't ashamed of being Ivy's husband.

Suddenly, he closed the drawer and the doors on the armoire. His mind made up, he picked up his jacket, stuck the box in his pocket and left the house.

He couldn't take it any longer. Even if she told him to go to hell or that she was going to get the annulment, at least he would hear the news in person.

With purpose and determination, Jonathan drove over to Ivy's house. He wouldn't let another day go by without resolving the situation. Not knowing where he stood in her life was brutal. He wanted to love her and to be loved by her. Once he left her house tonight, he'd have his answer.

Jumping out of the truck, he moved swiftly to the front door. He slipped his hands inside his jacket pocket, waiting for her to answer.

Just as Jonathan was about to ring the bell again, Ivy opened the door.

"Yes?" she said, her face blank and cold.

"Can I come in?"

"What do you want?"

"I want to talk to you."

"About?"

"Us. Let me come in and talk to you."

Several moments went by before she pushed the door open.

"Talk," she said, closing the door behind her.

Jonathan reached out to touch Ivy's arm, but she turned and walked around him.

Removing his jacket, he laid it on the arm of the sofa and sat down. Ivy treating him like a stranger stung, but he cleared his throat.

"Baby, come over here and sit next to me."

He knew Ivy was determined to hold on to her anger when she didn't move.

"Jonathan, you betrayed my trust."

"I did not betray you."

She threw up her hand. "Whatever, Jonathan, whatever."

"Hold on, you need to settle down." Jonathan stayed seated, but he really wanted to grab her and shake some sense into her head. "Let me ask you a question."

Ivy looked at him. "I'm listening."

"Have I ever lied to you?"

"No," she said, her voice barely above a whisper. She turned away so her eyes didn't meet his gaze.

Jonathan stood. "Haven't I supported you?"

"Yes."

Walking over to her, he reached out to her first to see if she would turn away. When she didn't, he turned her around so they could face each other.

Ivy dropped her head.

Jonathan continued.

"Did I ever mistreat you, disrespect you, or abuse you with words?"

Slowly, Ivy lifted her head; they stood silently staring at each other.

With sadness in her eyes, she swallowed hard before she answered. "No, you didn't."

Jonathan opened his arms to her, waiting for her to fill them.

Gradually, Ivy lifted her hand until it touched his. Jonathan grasped it securely. Leading her over to the sofa, they sat down together.

"Baby, I am sorry for putting our business out there like that. I know you're a private person, but Marc had made me so angry, I blurted it out."

"You had no right to do that."

"Oh, I did, because I'm in this with you as well."

Jonathan lifted her chin, gazing into her brown eyes. He said, "You have to know that I love and care for you. I told you that I'd always be there for you and, from the moment we got married, I've kept my promise to you."

"How can I trust you after what happened the other night?"

"You know what I think? All this frustration, anger and distrust are geared toward the wrong person."

Ivy quickly stood up. "Oh, I know who I'm angry at, Jonathan."

He stood up as well. "Ivy, I don't want you to get what I'm saying twisted. What I mean is that Randall is the person you're angry with, not me. I didn't betray your trust or make you feel unworthy or humiliate you. He did."

Ivy opened her mouth to retort, but Jonathan stopped her. "Wait, let me finish. Even though you said you both went your separate ways after the accident, I don't think you ever really dealt with your feelings about the situation."

Tears were rolling down Ivy's face; she was clearly upset by what he'd said. "How can you say that I didn't deal with Randall? It took me a long time to heal from that experience."

He caressed her cheek. "Baby, I want you to be honest with yourself. I think you started trying to deal with it when you told me about it. And that was only because he had shown up in the flesh."

Ivy turned away, but Jonathan followed. "I'm not trying to hurt you, baby. I'd never do anything that would bring harm to you. I'm your covering, and what kind of man would I be if I didn't treat my wife right?"

Walking back over to the sofa, Ivy sat down, resting with her head thrown back and her eyes closed. After releasing an exasperated breath, she sat up straight.

Jonathan still stood in front of her, and she patted the empty space next to her. He came over and sat down.

"When I came home from the hospital that day, I was so hurt and angry. I really thought he loved me, but in retrospect, it was always about him, what he wanted and how he wanted it to be."

She scooted closer to Jonathan. "You are right, I didn't deal with my feelings about how my relationship ended with Randall. It hurt so bad that I tried to ignore all those feelings."

Laying her head on Jonathan's shoulder, she said in a whisper, "You've been nothing but kind to me. I need you to be patient while I work some things out."

Jonathan placed a kiss on her head. "I'll be here for you. It's going to be all right."

At that moment, he decided it was time he found out where their marriage was headed. "Have you made a decision about us? Are we or aren't we going to stay together?"

Ivy sat up straight and turned toward him. "You are truly my friend, and what woman wouldn't want to be married to a man that loves, protects, cherishes, encourages and supports her every endeavor?" She pressed her fingers in his chest. "That's what you are to me, Jonathan."

Laying her head against his chest, they sat that way for a while before Jonathan spoke. "Does that mean you're not going back to Vegas?"

Ivy got up from the couch and left the room.

Jonathan tried to grab her hand, but she gently pulled it away and kept walking. "I want to get something," she said as she disappeared from his sight.

She returned with a familiar white envelope. She turned it upside down, and the gold ring that he'd purchased at the Las Vegas gift shop fell out. Ivy slid it on her finger.

Jonathan's heart sang a song of thanks. He lifted her hand. Kissing her knuckles, he said, "Baby, we're going to have to go and get you a real ring. I don't want your fingers turning green."

They both chuckled as Jonathan pulled her back into his arms. "Do you want to have a real wedding? Whatever you want, it's yours."

Ivy shook her head. "No, I think we should just have a reception. I don't want to ever forget how we got married."

"Yeah. I'll tell our children 'I wanted your momma so bad, I married her while she was drunk.' "

"You better not, Jonathan." Ivy couldn't help but laugh as well. She kissed his lips. "I love you, Mr. Damon."

"I love you, too, Mrs. Damon."

"Wait," Jonathan said, leaning over to the arm of the sofa, he picked up his jacket. He removed the blue velvet box.

Ivy's hand flew to her mouth. "You already bought me a ring?"

"No, baby, this isn't a ring. It's something very precious to me." He heard Ivy's gasp when he flipped open the lid.

He glanced up at her and could see tears forming in her eyes.

"It's beautiful," Ivy said, reaching out to touch the delicate piece of jewelry.

"This brooch belonged to my mother."

"Your mother?"

"Yes. She gave it to Aunt Rachel to give to me, along with this letter." Jonathan pulled the letter out of his other pocket and handed it to her.

Ivy skimmed the words on the sheet of paper. From time to time, she'd glance up at Jonathan. "This is so special. How long have you had this?"

"Aunt Rachel gave it to me the other day, along with this gift to give to my wife." Jonathan gave the box to Ivy, who had to clear her throat before she could speak.

"I don't know what to say." She couldn't form the words to express the way she felt about the gift. She'd never experienced something so beautiful and rare.

"You don't have to say anything; I just want you to give it to our daughter if we have a girl, or to our son to present to his wife one day."

"I will, I promise," Ivy said before she drew him close.

EPILOGUE

One year later . . .

Life for Ivy Hart Damon had changed so much, most importantly in her ability to love her husband without fear or inhibition. They were good together, and now with her reality show in its second season, life had definitely become more hectic.

Today, her sisters were throwing her a special viewing party for the premiere of *Here Comes The Bride—Chicago with Ivy Hart.*

Rose had given birth to a beautiful baby girl, Joi Marie. Ivy and Jonathan were asked to be her godparents. Joi was a good baby, and if Ivy could keep herself from picking her up every time she got a chance, she would stay that way.

Since both Joi's mommy and daddy were working, Ivy and Jonathan had to care for her. As she stood over the bed watching her goddaughter sleeping, Jonathan walked up behind her. "You know, Joi is just as beautiful as her god-mother," he said, kissing her softly on the nape of her neck. "Are you ready?"

"Yes, but I hate to wake her. She's sleeping so soundly."

"Baby, I can't believe that you're not worried about the time."

Glancing at the clock on the wall, Ivy said, "We've still got a little time yet." She left the room to get the jacket to her outfit. When she returned, Jonathan was holding Joi Marie.

"Jonathan, you are just as bad as Momma. You're going to spoil her."

"That's okay," he whispered. "An uncle has to spoil his goddaughter."

"Do you think I look okay?" Ivy asked, turning around in the burgundy, two-piece crinkled iridescent taffeta outfit.

"You look stunning, as always. Don't be nervous, baby."

"Okay, Papa, let's go," she said, grabbing the baby bag and her purse. She smiled as she watched how carefully Jonathan handled Joi, acting as if she was a piece of fine glassware.

Ivy couldn't wait until they had children of their own. Jonathan was going to be a great father.

Ivy stepped into the ballroom of Magic Moments and could not believe her eyes. Large displays were on the easels all around the room, all covered with satin drape. Rose had decorated the place, transforming it into a chic party place. As always, Ivy was impressed with her sister's creativity.

They even had a beautiful bassinet placed next to the dais for Joi.

At some point, Ivy realized that the guests included former clients who had brought their relatives and friends. And they were all making congratulatory remarks to her.

Rose and Marc came into the ballroom and headed straight for Ivy.

Rose was coming to get Joi, who had fallen asleep.

She bent over and lifted her baby girl up and placed her on her shoulder. She then leaned forward and kissed Ivy on the cheek.

"Hey, Vee. You know I had to come and get my baby before Momma got here."

Ivy smiled. Her niece would never want for love. She moved closer to her sisters. "Why are so many of our former clients here? I thought this was going to be a family affair."

Rose winked at her sister and turned to walk away. Looking back, she said, "We should be starting in a minute; you better take your seat."

Violet came to the podium.

"Good afternoon, ladies and gentlemen. We would like to thank you for coming out to celebrate the premiere of the second season of *Here Comes the Bride—Chicago*. In just a few moments we will preview this season's premiere episode, but first my brother-in-law Jonathan would like to have a few words."

"Good afternoon, everyone."

He then looked over at Ivy. "Baby, come over here."

Ivy got up from her seat smiling, filled with excitement. They had been married over a year and she couldn't have been happier with him. He still possessed all the same qualities, and had never wavered from his love for her.

A giddy feeling swept over Ivy as she watched him struggle to reach inside his jacket and hold the microphone at the same time. Finally, he handed her the mike, then reached in his jacket and removed a black velvet box.

Ivy's mouth dropped. Jonathan had just purchased a diamond wedding band to replace the plain gold one that they used for the ceremony when they got married. She tucked that one in a keepsake box along with their vanity marriage certificate.

Jonathan took the microphone from her and reached to grab her hand. "Baby, I'm so proud of you and what you've accomplished. You are so passionate about your work and about making wedding dreams a reality. I wanted to give you a small token of my love and affection." He steadied the mike and opened the box.

The site of the gorgeous platinum three-stone ring almost took her breath away. The beautifully crafted round center stone sparkled with the two shield-shape diamonds on the side.

Speechless, Ivy held out her hand. Jonathan slid the ring on her ring finger, where it nestled next to the diamond ring she was already wearing. Then, the ring in place, he kissed her.

Once he ended the kiss, Ivy started back to her seat, but he stopped her. "Hold on, baby, I'm not done with you yet." He signaled to the server in the back and the doors opened.

Lili rolled in a Las Vegas-themed three-tiered wedding cake. The middle tier had Ivy and Jonathan's names written around it in script.

Jonathan pulled Ivy into his arms. "I know our anniversary has passed, but I knew your sisters were throwing you this party, so I decided everyone here would celebrate our one year anniversary with us."

Lili stood next to the cake, beaming with pride in her creation. Ivy blew her a kiss and mouthed the words "thank you."

Turning her attention back to her husband, she took his face between her hands. "Happy anniversary, Mr. Damon," she said, leaning forward to lightly kiss his lips.

Jonathan stepped back and presented his wife to the audience. "I've loved her from the moment our eyes connected."

DEAR READER,

Thank you so much for reading Ivy and Jonathan's story. I pray that you enjoyed Ivy's roller coaster ride to forgiveness and true love.

People go through so many things in this life that leave them scarred, feeling guilty and sometimes causing them to build a wall when it comes to matters of the heart. It's a blessing when you find someone who will accept you as you are and love you anyway. That's what I admired so much about Jonathan Damon. To me it's unconditional love; something that is hard to find in this microwave society. Everyone is quick to judge even without thinking of their own faults, failures, and flaws.

I'm always happy to hear from readers. You can drop me a line at *seanyoung0907@msn.com* or go to my website *http://www.seanyoung.com.*

All good things in love and life,
Sean D. Young

Wedding Tip: In today's economy, everyone wants to cut costs. You can be realistic when planning your wedding without sacrificing your wedding dreams. Instead of getting married on a Saturday afternoon with a seven course dinner reception, plan a Friday evening or Sunday afternoon wedding serving brunch or lunch reception instead. Reception costs can account for up to 45% of your wedding budget.

2011 Mass Market Titles

January

From This Moment
Sean Young
ISBN: 978-1-58571-383-7
$6.99

Nihon Nights
Trisha Haddad and Monica
    Haddad
ISBN: 978-1-58571-382-0
$6.99

February

The Davis Years
Nicole Green
ISBN: 978-1-58571-390-5
$6.99

Allegro
Patricia Knight
ISBN: 978-158571-391-2
$6.99

March

Lies in Disguise
Bernice Layton
ISBN: 978-1-58571-392-9
$6.99

Steady
Ruthie Robinson
ISBN: 978-1-58571-393-6
$6.99

April

The Right Maneuver
LaShell Stratton-Childers
ISBN: 978-1-58571-394-3
$6.99

Riding the Corporate Ladder
Keith Walker
ISBN: 978-1-58571-395-0
$6.99

May

Separate Dreams
Joan Early
ISBN: 978-1-58571-434-6
$6.99

I Take This Woman
Chamein Canton
ISBN: 978-1-58571-435-3
$6.99

June

Doesn't Really Matter
Keisha Mennefee
ISBN: 978-1-58571-434-0
$6.99

Inside Out
Grayson Cole
ISBN: 978-1-58571-437-7
$6.99

2011 Mass Market Titles (continued)
July

Rehoboth Road
Anita Ballard-Jones
ISBN: 978-1-58571-438-4
$6.99

Holding Her Breath
Nicole Green
ISBN: 978-1-58571-439-1
$6.99

August

The Sea of Aaron
Kymberly Hunt
ISBN: 978-1-58571-440-7
$6.99d

The Finley Sisters' Oath of
    Romance
Keith Thomas Walker
ISBN: 978-1-58571-441-4
$6.99

September

October

November

December

Other Genesis Press, Inc. Titles

Other Genesis Press, Inc. Titles (continued)

Other Genesis Press, Inc. Titles (continued)

Other Genesis Press, Inc. Titles (continued)

How to Write a Romance	Kathryn Falk	$18.95
I Married a Reclining Chair	Lisa M. Fuhs	$8.95
I'll Be Your Shelter	Giselle Carmichael	$8.95
I'll Paint a Sun	A.J. Garrotto	$9.95
Icie	Pamela Leigh Starr	$8.95
If I Were Your Woman	LaConnie Taylor-Jones	$6.99
Illusions	Pamela Leigh Starr	$8.95
Indigo After Dark Vol. I	Nia Dixon/Angelique	$10.95
Indigo After Dark Vol. II	Dolores Bundy/ Cole Riley	$10.95
Indigo After Dark Vol. III	Montana Blue/ Coco Morena	$10.95
Indigo After Dark Vol. IV	Cassandra Colt/	$14.95
Indigo After Dark Vol. V	Delilah Dawson	$14.95
Indiscretions	Donna Hill	$8.95
Intentional Mistakes	Michele Sudler	$9.95
Interlude	Donna Hill	$8.95
Intimate Intentions	Angie Daniels	$8.95
It's in the Rhythm	Sammie Ward	$6.99
It's Not Over Yet	J.J. Michael	$9.95
Jolie's Surrender	Edwina Martin-Arnold	$8.95
Kiss or Keep	Debra Phillips	$8.95
Lace	Giselle Carmichael	$9.95
Lady Preacher	K.T. Richey	$6.99
Last Train to Memphis	Elsa Cook	$12.95
Lasting Valor	Ken Olsen	$24.95
Let Us Prey	Hunter Lundy	$25.95
Let's Get It On	Dyanne Davis	$6.99
Lies Too Long	Pamela Ridley	$13.95
Life Is Never As It Seems	J.J. Michael	$12.95
Lighter Shade of Brown	Vicki Andrews	$8.95
Look Both Ways	Joan Early	$6.99
Looking for Lily	Africa Fine	$6.99
Love Always	Mildred E. Riley	$10.95
Love Doesn't Come Easy	Charlyne Dickerson	$8.95
Love Out of Order	Nicole Green	$6.99
Love Unveiled	Gloria Greene	$10.95
Love's Deception	Charlene Berry	$10.95
Love's Destiny	M. Loui Quezada	$8.95
Love's Secrets	Yolanda McVey	$6.99

Other Genesis Press, Inc. Titles (continued)

Other Genesis Press, Inc. Titles (continued)

Other Genesis Press, Inc. Titles (continued)

Other Genesis Press, Inc. Titles (continued)

ESCAPE WITH INDIGO !!!!

Join Indigo Book Club©
It's simple, easy and secure.

Sign up and receive the new
releases
every month + Free shipping
and
20% off the cover price.

Visit us online at
www.genesis-press.com or
call 1-888-INDIGO-1